HUSH SONG

THE FIRST DREAM

Lianne Adams

ISBN-13: 979-8-9931483-1-1

Cover design by: Lianne Adams
Library of Congress Control Number: 2018675309
Printed in the United States of America

I want to thank my faithful Beta Readers:
Karen Lami (Author of Ember's Fire)
David Richards (Visual Artist an Writer)

CONTENTS

CHAPTER 1

The Riverlow

N'Kai's village curved gently around braided streams and reed-thick ponds. The air hung damp, laced with elder herbs and pollen. Homes nestled into the land, half-dug and half-woven, more root than wall. Mornings carried the scent of peat smoke and slow-boiling fruit; evenings settled with hush songs sung from hillside to hearth.

The hush songs still rose each night, but N'Kai no longer sang. He listened instead, to the quiet between verses.

He was coming of age. His voice had deepened, his walk sharpened, and even the water's edge no longer reflected a boy. In Riverlow, the passage into manhood arrived without fire or feast, without loud announcements or tribal drums. It came in the threading of suggestions, in the weight of silences, in the way mothers began to speak of daughters as if naming the future.

Ma'ren, his mother, wove her hopes into conversation like driftwood into a basket. One morning, while grinding riverroot, she mentioned the girl near the marsh who held good harvest lines. Later that week, as they mended nets, she spoke of the potter's daughter, noting her strong shoulders with the careful tone of someone planting a seed.

N'Kai listened. But the names fell into him like stones into deep water. No ripple. Just a gathering stillness.

Did he want the potter's daughter? The question sat in his chest like an unswallowed breath. Or did he only want to want her, to feel the pull Ma'ren seemed to expect? His ribs felt too tight, his skin too aware of itself, as if his body knew something his mind refused to name.

That dusk, he wandered beyond the woven paths and into the reeds. The mud sucked gently at his feet, cool and slick, releasing him with soft sighs. A reed brushed his wrist, dry and whispering. Light folded soft over the water, turning the surface to hammered bronze. A heron stood sleeping near the bank, one leg lifted, its stillness so complete it seemed carved from dusk itself. Dragonflies hummed low and blue, their wings catching the last light.

The hush song drifted from the hillside, slower

now, as if the land itself strained to remember. Beneath the reeds, a shifting sound rose: mud sighing, roots moving, something alive but unseen. A single frog barked in the dusk. Then silence. Then a willow branch stirred without wind.

He knelt. Touched the muddy root of the willow. A vibration curled through his palm, faint like a memory unspoken. Something flickered inside him. Not a thought, not yet. More like the twitch of a muscle before movement, the catch of breath before speech.

His palm pressed harder against the root, and the vibration answered: a pulse that traveled up his wrist, into his forearm, settling somewhere behind his ribs. It felt like recognition without image, like his body remembering something it had never learned.

There was a waiting in him now. Not patient, not restless, just present. Like water gathering behind a dam, like seed-weight in dark soil. A shape he couldn't name but could feel forming, the way morning fog takes form before you can see through it.

He stayed kneeling until the light failed completely, until the heron woke and lifted into darkness, until even the willow seemed to lean away, releasing him.

When he finally stood, his legs ached from stillness, but something else ached too, deeper and unnamed, insistent as hunger but softer than want.

A shadow not yet met. A door not yet opened.

But waiting.

CHAPTER 2

The Threading

Ma'ren hummed the hush song slower than usual, her voice thin as smoke drifting from the evening fires. She had sung it since she was twelve, the notes braided so deeply with firewood gathering and the comfort of forgetting that she could hardly separate the melody from the memories it carried. The song was meant to ward off the dark, to wrap the village in a blanket of familiar sound as night settled over the reeds and ponds.

But as the melody leaned into its final turn, she paused. Her breath caught in her throat. A tremor ran through her chest, subtle but unmistakable. The rhythm had shifted beneath her voice, not wrong exactly, but stretched, like a thread pulled so taut it might snap at any moment.

Ma'ren frowned and listened harder, letting the

song fade from her lips. The hush song had never changed before; it was as constant as the river's flow, as reliable as the seasons. Yet tonight something felt different. Another song seemed to thread through hers from the edges, older and quieter, tugging at corners of her memory she couldn't quite reach.

She stepped past the woven threshold of her home, her heart thudding against her ribs. The evening air pressed cool against her skin as she stood listening.

The frogs stopped their chorus.

The reeds whispered secrets to each other in the windless air.

And the wind itself, she could have sworn, curled around a name she didn't yet know, carrying it just beyond the reach of understanding.

Ma'ren shivered despite the warmth still radiating from the earth. The hush song had always been hers, a tether anchoring her to the world she knew, to the traditions passed down through generations of her people. But standing there in the threshold between firelight and darkness, she felt it transform. The song was no longer just a comfort or a ritual.

It had become a door.

She remained motionless, barely breathing, waiting for whatever lay beyond to reveal itself.

CHAPTER 3

The Wanting Season

N'Kai's body was speaking louder than ritual now, though not with rebellion. It spoke with resonance—a deep vibration that hummed beneath his skin and refused to be ignored.

He woke hungry sometimes, wide-eyed in the darkness with his breath coming shallow and quick. His dreams were slick with forms he couldn't name, only feel. He dreamed of breath hot against bark, of fingers trailing through moving water, of a mouth opening not to speak but to invite. He didn't know whose touch he waited for in those dream-soaked hours before dawn. He only knew that his skin had begun listening—not to words, but to warmth, to weight, to the way silence pressed against him.

The hush songs no longer settled him the way they once had. They used to tuck his soul in tight like wool, like moss, like memory itself.

Now they curled around the hearth while he lay awake, each note a thread pulling taut against something loosening inside him. He didn't know why they no longer soothed him and couldn't name the moment when their comfort had transformed into a kind of ache. He only knew the change had happened, as inevitable as the deepening of his voice.

He found himself noticing things he'd never paid attention to before. The curve of shoulders. The way laughter folded into gesture, becoming something more than sound. The way hands paused mid-air, as if remembering something they hadn't yet touched. He watched mouths and the silence that surrounded them, watched the space between words where meaning gathered like morning mist over the river.

This watching wasn't quite lust, though desire threaded through it. It felt more like invitation—not just to enter someone else's world, but to be entered, rewritten, seen through. He wanted recognition, not for legacy or lineage, but for want itself. Something in him was being called forward, a self he couldn't yet name. Not a name bestowed by elders or ritual, but one discovered in the soft grammar of longing, in the way breath caught when no one was watching.

He wanted to walk past the mapped hills. He wanted to kneel before stones with no lineage pressed into them, to sleep beneath a sky that didn't echo his grandfather's name in the wind. He wanted to laugh in places where no one knew his name meant "still water," where his steps didn't mirror Ma'ren's familiar rhythm, where memory didn't dress him in meanings that belonged to someone else's story.

He wanted to unmoor himself—gently, without violence—to loosen the thread between root and ritual without tearing it completely. He wanted to bloom not from heritage but from hunger, to become not what he was told to be or what the hush songs named, but what his own body was slowly remembering.

A shape without script. A story with no elder footnote. Something unnamed and utterly true.

CHAPTER 4

The Gathering Place

N'Kai and his closest friends—Jori, Tam, and Asho—gathered at a bend in the woods where the river split into braided streams. The place wasn't marked on any elder map. It belonged only to them, a secret kept without effort simply because no adult thought to follow where barefoot boys disappeared.

A natural hollow nestled there among the splitleaf trees, and sunlight poured through the canopy in golden shafts that sifted dust across their backs. Moss grew thick on the stones, making soft cushions that stayed cool even in midsummer's heat. The place smelled of mint and rain rot and old fish—like something caught between living and forgetting. The river whispered as it slipped over smooth rocks, a constant hush that seemed to carry secrets in its current. The air hung damp and sweet, tinged with the green breath of moss and the lingering memory of yesterday's rain.

They came barefoot and dream-minded, their pockets and pouches filled with the currency of boyhood—jars for catching fireflies, knives dulled from carving, fruit stolen from home stores, and secrets they couldn't yet name.

They would settle on the moss and talk low, their voices pitched between serious and silly. They tossed words like stones into shallow water, meant to splash and ripple, never to wound.

"I want a woman who fights bears," Tam would declare, puffing out his chest. His voice always came a little too loud, as if he was trying to fill the silence before it could expose him.

"I want one who doesn't speak," Asho would counter with a grin that showed teeth sharp and uncertain. His words came clipped and quick, tumbling over each other as if afraid they might vanish before landing.

"I want one who sees me," N'Kai would offer quietly, his voice wondering. He didn't know exactly what he meant by that, only that the words tasted true on his tongue.

They carved their tiny hopes into bark, shaped their longing in crooked spirals that meant nothing to anyone but themselves. They whispered oaths into jars they'd filled with waterleaf and the strange glow of dusklight insects. Some jars they buried beneath the moss, marking the spots with stones only they would recognize. Others they let drift downstream, watching until the current carried them out of sight. And some wishes they never spoke aloud at all, only pressed them between palm and silence like flowers preserved in memory.

Jori, the quietest of them, would sometimes hum a tune no one else knew. Tam swore he heard it later in his dreams, though he could never quite remember it upon waking. Once, Asho tried to kiss the air, pretending it was a girl made entirely of wind. They laughed so hard their ribs ached, tears streaming down their faces, and they swore to each other they would never forget that moment.

Sometimes they abandoned words altogether and simply lay back on the moss to watch clouds move across the sky like vast herds migrating. They wondered aloud how far the clouds would travel before the wind changed its mind and scattered them in new directions.

N'Kai would think about how the river held their secrets without judgment, how the moss remembered the shape and weight of their bodies, how the stones never demanded answers to questions they weren't ready to face. He didn't know what kind of man he would become in the years ahead, but he knew with bone-deep certainty that this place would always be part of him—woven into whatever self he would eventually discover.

The hollow didn't ask who they would become. It only listened, and held, and became part of them in return—stone and moss and river and oath, all braided together like the streams that split and rejoined around them.

CHAPTER 5

Whispers at the Splitriver Hollow

The moss beneath N'Kai's elbows was damp and clinging, pressing into his skin like memory, itching like a warning he couldn't quite decipher. Tam lay sprawled across a sun-warmed stone nearby, chewing thoughtfully on a reed. Asho sat cross-legged with his eyes half-closed, wearing the expression of someone who'd already dreamed the ending of a story before it began.

"They're called the Others," Tam whispered, breaking the comfortable silence. "Not by name. Just... in stories."

"They live past the frostline," Asho added, his eyes still closed. "Where the mammoths left their bones and the berries grow mean and red."

"Where it's too cold to guard your daughters properly," Tam said with a smirk that didn't quite reach his eyes.

N'Kai didn't laugh. He was listening with the kind of attention that made everything else fade away, listening like it mattered, like the moss beneath them might remember every word spoken in this place.

The talk wasn't new. It trickled down from older boys like spring melt through the rocks, half-shaped, half-spoken, never entirely clean. Rumors of tundra women who walked alone without fear, who laughed too easily, who touched first instead of waiting to be chosen. Women who did the choosing themselves.

"My uncle says the girls there aren't locked up in harvest talk and stone-choosing ceremonies," Tam continued, warming to his subject. "They dance in the open, with anyone they please."

"Not a wife," Asho murmured, his lips curving into a small smile. "Just a good story to tell."

The wind rustled through the splitleaf trees above them, and N'Kai's mind drifted to Ma'ren's ritual whispering over the past weeks. She named potential matches like harvest predictions: strong shoulders, good hips, quiet mouths. All the qualities that made a suitable wife in Riverlow.

He couldn't picture himself marrying a quiet mouth. The thought sat wrong in his chest.

"They laugh," N'Kai said softly, testing the words. "That's what they say about them. They laugh without permission."

Tam blinked at him. Asho raised an eyebrow, both eyes open now.

"And they choose," N'Kai added, his voice barely above a whisper.

No one spoke for a long moment. The moss seemed to shift beneath them, as if it too was listening, bearing witness to this small rebellion of wanting something different.

Then Tam leaned in closer, his voice dropping even lower.

"There's another story," he said. "Not about the girls. About what watches them."

Asho snorted, but there was nervousness behind it. "You mean the A'ta?"

Tam nodded, his earlier bravado fading. "My cousin swears he saw one once. Said it was fog-thin, barely there. Eyes like mothlight, you know, that strange glow you see in the dark. He said it smiled at him, and afterward he forgot his own name for a week."

"They don't eat you," Asho said, as if reciting something he'd been told. "They just take your best memory and leave you smiling like you've been given a gift."

"Or worse," Tam added, his voice tight. "They give you someone else's memories. You wake up remembering things that never happened to you."

N'Kai felt a chill run through him, not from fear exactly, but from recognition. Something in him had already begun to loosen over these past weeks, like a thread pulled taut against a name he hadn't yet spoken aloud.

"They feed on longing," Tam whispered, and now all three boys were leaning in, caught in the gravity of the story. "That's what the old stories say. Not blood. Not flesh. Just the ache itself."

Asho tossed a pebble into the stream, watching the ripples spread. "Sounds like love," he said.

"Sounds like danger," Tam replied.

N'Kai looked down at the palm of his hand. A fresh nick marked his skin from carving in his barkstrip journal the night before. The small wound ached in a way that reminded him of the moss beneath him, of memory that wouldn't let go.

He thought to himself, with a clarity that surprised him: Maybe danger is the point.

CHAPTER 6

Ma'ren of the Riverlands

Ma'ren stood tall even when the wind bent the reeds around her, her breath steady against the gusts that swept across the wetlands. Her hair, long and grey, hung in a thick braid woven through with bone beads and smooth river-stones—each one a memory she had chosen to carry, not one given to her by obligation. As Elder of the Riverlands, keeper of hush songs and ledger knots, she shaped tradition with quiet hands and a gaze as sharp as frost on winter grass. She did not speak often, but when she did, the air itself seemed to still. Carving hands paused mid-motion. Even the gulls stopped their crying to listen. Her hands bore the ink-stains of a thousand trades recorded, and her voice carried the hush of winter wind through bare branches. Ma'ren did not command her people—she remembered for them. And in that remembering, she shaped everything and everyone she touched.

She watched N'Kai sketch spirals in the dirt beside their dwelling—always spirals, endless and turning. Even as a child, he had traced them everywhere: in steam rising from cook pots, in sand along the riverbank, in the dust that settled on her ledger table. She used to think it was simple mimicry, a child copying the patterns he saw in nature. Now she knew better. It was longing given shape. A form without end, turning and turning. He was her only son, and already she could sense him loosening, the threads that bound him to this place shifting in the quiet space between them.

She felt it in her knees when she rose from kneeling, in the weight of her braid against her back, in the way her breath caught when he asked what the fog meant. It rolled in thick and low some mornings, carrying the smell of wet stone and moss, muffling the gulls' cries and the river's constant chatter. He was listening differently now—not for instruction, but for invitation. Not asking what he should do, but what he might choose to do.

She remembered the day he first bled from carving, how young he'd been. He had clenched his small fists and refused to cry despite the pain. She had sung the hush song of the river's bend and pressed healing balm into his palms with steady fingers. She remembered the night he asked about the ancestors, wanting to know their names and stories. She had named them all for him, even the ones most people had forgotten—especially those ones, because someone needed to remember.

She knew he was choosing now, though he might not yet see it himself. He was choosing in the quiet way of river stones that shift beneath the surface—slow, certain, inevitable. The current moves them without drama or announcement, but move they do.

She would take him to the tundra. Not to protect him from what he might find there, and not to test whether he was worthy. She would take him to let him see what choosing looked like when it wasn't wrapped tight in ritual and expectation. The Others who lived beyond the frostline did not name their children with stone ceremonies or match girls to boys based on harvest predictions. They danced in the open. They laughed without asking permission. They chose their own paths.

She would take him because he was already walking toward something—not with defiance or rebellion, but with the quiet gravity of someone who had begun listening for a different rhythm beneath the familiar songs. She could see it in the way he watched the morning fog, in the way he carved his spirals deeper than tradition required, as if trying to tunnel through to some truth hidden below.

She would take him because she loved him—not with easy warmth or indulgent softness, but with the kind of love that tempers a child like metal in fire. The kind that prepares them for the ache of becoming someone new. The kind of love that teaches silence not as submission but as strength, that knows when to hold on and when to let go, even when the letting go aches like a wound.

And she would take him because one day, if he returned to Riverlow, he would be Elder. He would be keeper of hush songs and ledger knots, guardian of memory and forgetting both. Elders must understand what longing costs—not only the weight of story and ritual that everyone could see, but the ache beneath them that no one spoke of. The hunger that shapes memory. The danger and grace that come with choosing freely instead of following the path laid out by others.

Her fingers found the beads at her neck, touching them one by one: bone, riverstone, memory. She lingered on the smallest bead, the one she had knotted when he was born—his first cry breaking the silence, then his first profound silence when he finally slept. Soon, she knew, she would need to knot another bead onto her braid.

The day he stepped into the tundra and did not look back toward home.

CHAPTER 7

Hush-Song and Bone

The afternoon sun soaked the village in gold, stretching shadows long across the ground like old stories being told and retold. The air held the sweet tang of ripening riverfruit mixed with the damp hush of moss, as if the pond itself remembered yesterday's rain and held it close.

N'Kai sat cross-legged near the reed pond, sketching spirals onto a piece of bark with a sharpened stick. He wasn't thinking in words—only in shapes and movement, in the way something might turn and keep turning even after you stopped touching it, momentum carrying it forward into infinity.

Ma'ren approached without sound, as she always did. Her footsteps made no impression on the soft earth.

"You'll come with me," she said simply.

He looked up, squinting against the light behind her.

"For trade," she added before he could ask. "Dried root. Riverfruit. Balm-honey. You'll carry the ledger and keep the records. I'll do the speaking. You'll listen and learn."

N'Kai nodded slowly, setting down his carving stick.

"Where?" he asked.

She didn't answer immediately. Her gaze drifted past the water, past the fog-line where the well-worn path narrowed and disappeared into something less charted, less certain.

"To the tundra," she said finally, her eyes still fixed on that distant fog. "To the Others."

His chest fluttered—an involuntary tremor in bone and blood that he couldn't suppress. It felt like being chosen for something important. But also like choosing it himself, like the decision had already been made somewhere deep inside him before Ma'ren ever spoke the words.

Ma'ren knelt beside him, her fingers brushing the edge of the spiral he'd been carving. She traced the line with one weathered fingertip.

"There are stories," she said softly, her voice taking on the quality she used for important things. "Of women who laugh without asking permission. Of men who forget their own names and don't mind the forgetting."

N'Kai went very still, hardly breathing.

"They say the fog carries memory up there," she continued, her eyes distant. "And that something walks inside it. Not a beast exactly. Not a ghost. Just... hunger, given form and purpose."

He thought of Tam's whispered stories at the Splitriver Hollow. Of mothlight eyes and smiles that could rewrite you from the inside out.

Ma'ren's voice dropped lower, taking on the cadence of a hush-song—half melody, half warning, the kind of knowledge that had been passed down for generations.

"If you hear your name in the wind, don't answer," she said. "If you see your face reflected in still water, don't touch the surface. If you feel warmth where there should be only cold—run."

The words settled over him like a cloak. Ma'ren let the hush-song rhythm linger for a moment before her voice shifted, becoming lower and steadier, more practical.

"You'll see their homes," she said. "The tundra folk. They build from what remains after the great beasts fall."

N'Kai tilted his head, curious despite the warnings still echoing in his mind.

"Mammoth bone," Ma'ren explained. "They use curved tusks for arches over doorways. Ribcages become domed roofs. Massive femurs serve as lintels and support beams. People say the bones sing in the wind—low and hollow, as if the beasts themselves still breathe somewhere beneath the snow."

He blinked, trying to imagine it. He'd heard the stories all his life, as everyone had. But no one in Riverlow had seen a living mammoth in his lifetime, or his mother's, or even his grandmother's.

"The mammoths are nearly gone now," Ma'ren said, and something like sorrow crossed her face. "But they're not forgotten. Some say a few still walk the deep ice, in places where no path holds, where even the fog won't venture."

She paused, then added quietly, "If you hear thunder when there's no storm, it might be one of the last mammoths. Don't chase it. Let it pass in peace."

N'Kai swallowed hard, his throat suddenly dry.

"This is the warm season," Ma'ren said, her tone becoming more practical again. "The only warm season the tundra offers. And the crinwood berries will be thick now—so thick you'll crush them with every step you take."

He imagined it: red-gold berries bursting underfoot with each footfall, staining the ground like spilled flame, like blood from some small wound.

"They're prized up there," she said. "For winter food stores. For wine-making. For trade with outsiders. The seeds hold heat somehow, even after drying. And the juice holds memory."

N'Kai frowned at that. "Memory?"

He'd never tasted crinwood wine himself—it was far too valuable to waste on children. But he'd seen what it did to those who drank it. How it made old men weep for reasons they couldn't explain. How it made young ones forget their own names for hours afterward, walking around with dazed smiles.

Ma'ren's lips curved in a faint smile.

"Some say if you drink crinwood wine under a new moon, you'll dream of someone you've forgotten," she said. "Or perhaps of someone who's forgotten you."

She reached out and brushed a strand of hair from his brow with gentle fingers.

"We'll trade for some of the berries. But not too many. The tundra gives, but it watches everything it gives away. Best not to be greedy."

She stood then, brushing bits of moss from her knees. Her shadow stretched long across the bark spirals he'd been carving, making them look deeper, more complex.

"Pack light," she instructed. "Bring warm

clothes and a quiet heart. And bring silence with you—the fog up there listens to everything."

N'Kai watched her walk away, the fragments of hush-song still trailing behind her like visible thread in the golden air.

After she disappeared around the corner of a dwelling, he hummed the first line of the song under his breath. Not to help himself remember the warning.

To practice resisting its pull.

CHAPTER 8

Packing

N'Kai packed carefully that night—too carefully, with the kind of attention that made each fold feel like a farewell rather than simple preparation for travel.

As he worked, a part of him yearned to stay in Riverlow, to forget the tundra and the Others and simply remain in the only home he'd ever known. He laid each item on the woven mat as if it might speak to him, as if the objects themselves could tell him whether leaving was the right choice.

The riverroot bundles came first—dried and braided, still humming faintly with the scent of wet stone. Their smell reminded him of his friends gathered by the fire, of laughter and easy companionship. The bone-handled knife went next, honed sharp by his uncle's practiced hand, still bearing the small notch from last winter's hunt. It gleamed under the dim lamplight, its smooth surface cool and familiar against his palm.

And then the journal.

Barkstrips bound together with reed thread, each rough sheet inscribed with things he hadn't dared share with anyone. Spirals that went nowhere and everywhere. Dreams he couldn't quite remember upon waking but had tried to capture anyway. Names he'd never spoken aloud, belonging to feelings he couldn't yet articulate. Some pages were smudged with ash from sitting too close to the fire while he wrote. Others bore the marks of salt—whether from tears or sweat, he couldn't say.

He touched the journal's cover as if it might burn him. Or perhaps forgive him for the wanting written inside.

He packed everything into his satchel, then unpacked it all and started over. Then did it again, and again a third time, until he realized he was simply seeking comfort in the rhythm of folding and unfolding, in the familiar motions that kept his hands busy and his mind from racing ahead to what awaited.

The satchel felt heavier than it should when he finally finished. Not with physical weight, but with meaning—with the knowledge that these ordinary objects were crossing a threshold with him into something unknown.

Outside, the wind whispered its secrets through the trees, and he couldn't tell if it was warning him or encouraging him forward.

He sat on his sleeping mat for a long moment, knees drawn up to his chest, watching shadows move across the threshold as the lamp flame flickered. He didn't sleep that night—not really. He only drifted in and out of something like sleep, his pulse and his memories intertwining like shadows at dusk, impossible to separate.

The next morning arrived with a sky the color of river ice—blue, but bruised with darker currents running through it.

His friends met him near the Splitriver Hollow, where morning fog curled like breath around the familiar stones. They came with smirks and mock-heroics, their voices deliberately bright against the hush that had settled over everything.

"Bring back a wild wife," Tam called with a teasing grin, tossing him a small pouch of dried berries for the journey.

"Trade your silence for a laugh," Asho added, grinning as he tapped his own chest twice in the traditional gesture of farewell.

Jori flung his arms wide like antlers—mimicking the gesture they'd invented as children—but then added softly, his smile fading, "Just remember us when you're riding mammoths."

N'Kai smiled at them but found he couldn't form words in response. His thoughts were frost-bitten and fire-warmed all at once, pulling him in too many directions. He wanted to laugh with them one more time. He wanted to run away from this leaving. He wanted to stay forever in this moment, this place, with these people who knew him.

As he adjusted the satchel on his shoulder, an uneasy flutter stirred in his chest—a whisper that adventure awaited beyond the fog, yes, but so did uncertainty. So did change that couldn't be undone.

He nodded once to his friends, unable to trust his voice, and stepped away from the Hollow.

The fog parted before him.

Just slightly.

Just enough to show him the path forward.

CHAPTER 9

The Climb Toward the Others

The path out of Riverlow curved uphill like a question not yet asked.

It began with mud, wet and familiar. N'Kai's boots sank and sighed with every step, squelching softly as if the earth were reluctant to let go. The texture clung to his soles, thick and grainy, a memory made tangible. The air smelled of damp bark and pollen, soft in the lungs, as if the village didn't want him to leave. Even the wind clung to him like a shawl.

By midmorning, he passed the outer herbs, where Ma'ren's people gathered moss and minted leaf. He did not speak to them. They did not ask where he was going. They had already blessed him in silence, which, in Riverlow, was louder than drums.

The river lay low before him, flat as breath held too long, its surface a hush of silver and shadow.

Mist braided through the reeds, soft and stubborn. The air was thick with scent: fishskin, moss rot, the faint tang of iron where the water kissed stone. Beneath it all, a sweetness: riverfruit bruising in the shallows, balm-honey from Ma'ren's satchel clinging to his sleeve. The smells stirred memories: Ma'ren's voice, the hush of twilight songs, the warmth of shared stories.

N'Kai stepped lightly, each footfall sinking into mud that remembered. The ground gave way with a sigh, like it knew him.

He hummed a hush song, very quietly. Just the first few notes, barely more than breath.

It wasn't for anyone else. It was for the river. For the hollow. For the part of him that still listened.

The tune curled in the air like mist, unfinished and unclaimed. A rhythm of breath and silence. Of things not spoken but felt.

A heron lifted from the reeds, wings slicing the quiet. He watched it go, thinking: even flight left a shadow.

The ledger was tucked beneath his arm, pages soft with use. He would carry it across the frost-line. He would listen. He would choose what to remember. He would find what waited beyond the hush.

The river did not ask his name. It only offered stillness.

And N'Kai, for once, did not resist.

CHAPTER 10

The First Night

The fire burned low, just enough to keep frost from claiming their boots. Ma'ren lay wrapped in her tradecloak, eyes closed, breath steady. But she was not asleep.

N'Kai sat apart from her, his carved stick across his knees. The spiral caught firelight, glowing like a wound, raw yet beautiful. He had grown taller than she'd expected when she first packed for the journey. His shoulders had broadened. His jaw had begun to square.

But it was the way he moved that marked the shift. Deliberate, quiet, like someone who'd learned to listen before speaking. His hair hung dark and wind-tangled, left loose in the style of young Riverlands men. A symbol of freedom he embraced without flaunting. When his eyes had caught hers earlier, they'd held something unreadable. Not defiance. Not obedience. Something in between, a silent rebellion against expectations.

He began to sing.

Softly.

A hush song, but not one she'd taught him. The melody curled like smoke through the cold air, low and reed-thin, barely louder than the wind. She'd known since he was small that he was a good singer. But he seldom sang loudly. His voice was a dusk voice. A fog voice. The kind that asked permission without words.

Ma'ren kept her eyes closed. She let the song braid itself around her breath, let the silence between verses speak what he could not. He thought she was asleep, and so he sang freely.

In that moment, she saw him clearly. Not just the boy she'd raised, but the man he was becoming. Respectful. Rebellious. Listening. Choosing.

Her fingers found the bead at her neck, the one for his first silence, and lingered there. She waited for the next.

CHAPTER 11

The Slow Altering

The world didn't shatter or roar. It merely shifted in silence, through quiet refusals rather than thunder. A bird no longer sang, leaving the air hollow. A path no longer welcomed, its edges brittle. Warmth withdrew like breath withheld. These changes seemed like nothing until they had already reshaped you, the kind that seeped beneath the skin, altering your rhythm before you realized you'd begun to walk differently.

Day One: The Crossing Begins

Green faded. The color retreated in patches, like old bark lifting from wood, like memory retreating from the edges of a dream. The moss dulled first, then the ferns. Even the riverleaf lost its shimmer, curling inward as if bracing for something unnamed. Stone veins curled through the soil like old scars surfacing, present and undeniable, though neither fresh nor bleeding. The kind of truth that waited in silence to be noticed.

The birds grew quiet. They hadn't gone, only grown watchful. Their wings tucked tighter. Their eyes followed the travelers without blinking. Even the air seemed to listen.

N'Kai felt the hush settle in his chest like a held breath. The sensation carried no fear, only the particular silence that came before a story began, or before a name changed. He didn't ask where they were going. The question had already passed through him days ago, like a fever. He knew now their destination was a crossing, a shift in the marrow, a loosening of the old self.

He adjusted the strap of his satchel, felt the weight of balm oil and spiral carvings press against his side. He walked behind Ma'ren, who didn't speak either. The path narrowed. The trees leaned in. A branch cracked in the distance, sharp, deliberate. He paused, breath held. Ma'ren glanced back, her eyes steady, then turned forward again. And the world had already changed beneath his feet.

Day Two: The Bone-Sung Wind

The wind began to hum in a pitch he couldn't name, something like distant singing through bone, beyond music or warning. A vibration that bypassed the ears and settled deep in the ribs, thrumming against his breastbone like a second heartbeat. It made him feel hollow and tuned, like something inside him had been strung for resonance.

The wind carried the dry scent of cedar and ash, mingled with something sharper underneath: the mineral bite of glacial dust, the faint sweetness of frozen lichen crushed underfoot. It pressed against his exposed skin with a cold that didn't simply touch but penetrated, numbing his cheeks and making his eyes water. When it gusted, it tugged at his cloak with invisible fingers, flattening the grass around them in silver waves that rippled toward the horizon. The sound rose and fell, a moan caught between the rocks, threading through gaps in stone with a voice that seemed almost deliberate.

He walked with Ma'ren and two elders. Their steps were deliberate, unhurried. The bundles they carried were wrapped in riverleaf, green veined with silver, folded with reverence. Inside were herbs for healing, dried fruits for sustenance, spiral carvings etched with memory, and balm oil sealed in barkskin, still fragrant with cedar and ash. Trade gifts. Ritual gifts. Truth softened and made palatable, perhaps disguised as barter, or perhaps simply offered gently.

Each item held meaning. The herbs were remedies passed through generations. The fruits preserved sweetness from summer's end. The carvings were stories etched in spiral form. The balm offered protection, remembrance.

N'Kai watched the way the elders held their bundles, cradling them like mourners carrying offerings to a grave, or midwives bearing something newly born. He wondered what part of him was being offered. His body remained his own; he was still walking, still breathing. His voice too, though he hadn't spoken since the frost. Yet something was being carried forward, something he hadn't named but which the wind seemed to recognize.

He felt it in the way Ma'ren glanced at him, her gaze holding knowledge and quiet certainty, as if she'd already seen the shape he was becoming, as if she'd helped carve it. The wind shifted again, brushing his cheek like a thumbprint pressed into clay. He didn't flinch, but he did wonder if the wind was choosing him or simply remembering him, and if the world had already begun to barter with his silence.

CHAPTER 12

The Arrival

The first thing N'Kai noticed was the bones.

They weren't scattered like casualties of hunting seasons or buried beneath respectful earth. They had risen. Mammoth ribs arched overhead like cathedral spines, weatherworn but warm, their curves offering more than shelter. They held memory itself, visible and tangible in every graceful bend.

The bones framed everything: windbreaks that channeled the bitter air away from doorways, hearths where families gathered against the cold, thresholds that marked the passage from wilderness to home, resting places where elders sat and stories were told. Each rib bore the polish of generations—smoothed by countless hands, scoured by storms, burnished by the weight of stories pressed into their surface like prayers.

Smoke ribboned from flint-stone hearths, twisting upward in slow, deliberate spirals. It carried the scent of tart berries mingled with tallow-soaked moss, and beneath those familiar smells lay something older—a sweetness that had fermented in the cold, like fruit preserved beyond its season.

The ground beneath his boots crunched with each step. Frost lay everywhere, yet the sound came from something else: old memory compressed into the earth—shells, bark, bone fragments, all softened by time and retold by countless footsteps. The very soil seemed woven from the village's history.

The village pulsed with life. It was truly alive in a way Riverlow had never been, beyond mere occupation. Children ran barefoot across snow-kissed rock, their feet pattering like rain on stone, shouting in a tongue full of inflection and playful sound. Their words bounced like drumbeats off the curved ribs of the shelters, echoing and multiplying until the whole village seemed to ring with their joy.

Women laughed as they worked, their voices skipping like stones across still water. The sound wasn't careful or hushed, wasn't restrained by ritual or expectation. They laughed with the full-throated joy of people who owned their own rhythm, who shaped their days by choice rather than tradition.

Even the silence here felt different. It held no

tension, carried no weight of things unspoken. This was the kind of quiet that came after a song —satisfied rather than expectant, content rather than waiting.

Ma'ren bowed to the elders near the gate, her hands open in the universal gesture of peaceful intent. Her voice remained steady as she began the ritual greetings in trade tongue, each phrase shaped like a gift, offered with the careful dignity she brought to every formal exchange.

N'Kai followed her lead, adjusting the satchel at his side. His fingers brushed against the bark-strip journal tucked within—a tether to the journey they'd just completed, to the questions he hadn't yet found words to write down. The familiar texture grounded him as his eyes tried to absorb everything at once.

And then he truly looked.

He looked beyond the path Ma'ren was leading him down, beyond the village as a collection of structures and people. He looked into it—into the curve of the bone shelters and the rhythm of the voices, into the way the wind didn't fight against the structures but danced with them, weaving through gaps and around corners as if it had always belonged here.

He looked, and something looked back.

The place itself seemed to see him, to take his

measure with the patience of ancient bones and well-worn paths. It recognized him as someone beginning, someone at the threshold of becoming something he couldn't yet name—a stranger, yes, though perhaps someday he might be kin.

In that moment, N'Kai felt the ache return. The same ache that had driven him from Riverlow, that had whispered through the hush songs and called him beyond the mapped hills. Now it had a shape—curved like bone, open like an arch, unfinished like a question waiting for an answer.

This was the ache of becoming. And this place, with its memory-laden bones and joyful voices, had already begun to name him before he knew what name he would carry.

CHAPTER 13

Feeding the Fire

"NO, you cannot lick the ladle!" Elen bellowed, her laughter rolling through the hut as she swatted her son's hand with the hem of her hide apron. "You think stew tastes better off bark than bowl? Fool child!"

The hut shook with noise. Children squealed, bowls clanked against each other, and Elen's voice rose above it all like birds startled from the canopy. The air hung thick with the scent of simmering root stew—earthy and spiced, the aroma mingling with the musk of damp wood and smoke that clung to everything. The walls, curved and pale with mammoth bone, glowed amber in the firelight. Even the floor seemed to tremble with the weight of so much joy crammed into one small space.

Asha worked beside her mother, passing food with the fluid motions she'd learned since childhood. Elen roared stories and threats in equal measure, her voice never pausing, never softening. Asha found herself mimicking her mother's gestures without thinking—wiping a smear of stew from a child's cheek, tossing a bowl with the same practiced flair. Her fingers moved with grace, but her thoughts kept stuttering, wandering away from the warmth of the hearth.

Elen was built broad and solid, her hair braided thick around bone pins that clicked softly when she moved. Her laugh was as guttural as her grief was sharp—everything about her existed at full volume. She wiped stew from a toddler's eye with one hand while gesturing wildly with the other, painting the air with memories and warnings as if her words could take physical shape.

"Don't eat like you're starving unless you are!" she declared, pointing her serving spoon at the assembled children like a weapon. "Leave some for the moon spirits, or they'll steal your breath in sleep!"

The children cackled at the threat, delighted by the familiar warning. Asha rolled her eyes, but fondly, her lips twitching with a smile she didn't quite let bloom. She admired her mother's fire, even when it spilled over and scorched everything nearby. But today, Asha found herself quieter than usual, her mind roaming despite her hands' steady work.

Her thoughts circled between Bran's stone

gaze that made her feel both seen and judged, Turo's words that skipped and danced like wind through leaves, and Meko's gaze that lingered too long, heavy with something he never quite spoke aloud.

Her mother noticed. Elen noticed everything.

"Which boy is carving trails in your brain today?" she boomed, elbowing Asha with a grin that said she already knew the answer.

Asha flushed, heat creeping up her neck. "None."

"Lie louder, girl." Elen's grin widened. "I've given birth to seven and raised ten—you think I can't hear a heart pacing?"

She tossed a bowl toward her eldest son without even looking. He caught it one-handed while balancing a crying child on his hip, the movement so practiced it seemed effortless. The meal continued, wild and warm, voices layering over each other in comfortable chaos. But something had shifted in the air between mother and daughter.

Asha wasn't just thinking of the boys anymore. She was wondering if any of them could stand beside her mother and not shrink. She was wondering what kind of fire she carried inside herself, and whether it could ever burn as brightly as Elen's did.

Outside, the wind pressed against the curved walls of the hut like a curious hand testing for weaknesses. Inside, the stew bubbled on, fragrant and steady, while the family ate and argued and laughed around the fire.

CHAPTER 14

Tale by the Fire: Her Mother's Choosing

The question her mother had asked that evening, "Which boy is carving trails in your brain today?", refused to leave Asha alone. It followed her through the meal, through the washing of bowls, through the settling of younger siblings into their sleeping furs. Even now, with the hut finally quiet and the children breathing slow and deep around her, the question circled like smoke that wouldn't rise.

Asha sat braiding moss into rope for the fishing baskets, her fingers working by memory while her thoughts wandered elsewhere. Her mother sat cross-legged across the dying fire, watching the embers with an expression Asha rarely saw: something softer than her usual sharpness, edged with what might have been remembering.

Elen spat into the fire for punctuation, the way

she always did before saying something that mattered. The flames hissed and danced, casting flickering shadows across their faces. The scent of moss and smoke mingled in the air, earthy and sharp.

"I almost chose a man who could not hold a spear properly," she began, her voice dropping to a rumble like distant thunder. "Why? Because he smiled at me like he'd swallowed honey and wanted me to taste it."

Asha's hands stilled on the rope. She recognized this tone. Her mother was offering something rare: a glimpse backward, into the woman she'd been before children and duties and the weight of keeping everyone fed.

"Then your uncle challenged him to a game of bone-dodge," her mother continued, her eyes still fixed on the embers as though she could see the scene playing out in the coals. "You know that game?"

Asha nodded. "Fast. Brutal. Honest."

"That man dodged like tree bark. Got hit in the teeth."

Elen laughed, the sound erupting loud enough that one of the children stirred in their sleep. She lowered her voice, but the mirth remained. "When he fell, he cried like a squirrel. I left him that night. Chose your father instead. He never dodged. He charged."

Asha's brow furrowed. She thought of the boys in the village, the ones who smiled too easily or flinched at loud noises. She wondered what it meant to choose someone who charged.

Then her mother looked up from the fire, meeting Asha's eyes directly. When she spoke again, her voice had changed, the laughter gone, replaced by something that twisted deeper than any stew ladle ever could.

"Choosing isn't about liking someone. It's about who you want beside you when the winter stars scream and no one sleeps."

The words settled into Asha's chest like embers pressed against skin. She didn't know yet who she would choose, but she knew she wanted someone who wouldn't run.

The fire crackled softly between them, filling the silence. Her mother's gaze drifted back to the coals, and slowly the softness faded from her face, replaced by the familiar set of her jaw. The moment had passed. The glimpse backward had closed.

Asha returned to her braiding, but the rope felt different now, the fibers rough against fingers that had learned something new about her mother, about choosing, about the kind of strength that had nothing to do with volume.

Later, in the hush before dawn, Asha found herself awake while the rest of the hut slept on. She turned onto her side and watched her mother in the dim gray light. Loud as Elen was by day, now she lay curled around the youngest child, snoring softly, one hand twitching like it still shaped fire even in dreams.

Asha studied her mother's brow, the deep lines carved from years of fury and care, and whispered to the stars visible through the smoke hole above:

"I know how loud you are. But I wonder what you would've said, if silence hadn't frightened you more than solitude."

She thought of the fire, of the moss rough between her fingers, of the way her mother's voice had cracked like kindling when she spoke of choosing. She didn't want to be louder.

She wanted to be understood without needing to shout.

Sleep found her eventually, carrying her toward morning with the scent of cold embers and her mother's story woven through her dreams.

CHAPTER 15

Family Chaos Ritual: The Roar of Memory

It was tradition, once a moon cycle, for every child to wear something ridiculous—feathers in ears, mud patterns on cheeks—and scream their favorite memory at the sky. The sky was streaked with orange and violet, and the air buzzed with laughter and the scent of roasted squirrel.

Her mother started it years ago.

Now, it was riotous.

Asha stood in the middle as children twirled, shouted about honey-stealing, and imitation fights. One child yelled, "I once stole a whole honeycomb and blamed the dog!" Another spun in circles, chanting, "Mud warriors never lose!"

Her mother shouted her favorite memory—giving birth to twins while gnawing on roasted squirrel.

"I didn't drop a single bone!" she declared.

Asha laughed, but hers was quieter, more reflective.

Her memory?

"Mammoth hunt!" she cried, laughing.

She had convinced the small children that a mammoth lived just over the hill, then led a solemn expedition with sticks and berry rations to find it. She remembered the hush of their footsteps, the weight of her stick, the way the wind seemed to whisper approval, and the wide-eyed belief in every face. She had drawn mammoth tracks in the dirt and whispered tales of its tusks made of moonlight.

Her mother had winked at her afterward, saying, "You're the best kind of troublemaker."

Asha smiled at the memory, a mix of pride and longing curling in her chest.

These rituals, loud and absurd, stitched their family together—each shout a thread in the tapestry of who they were.

CHAPTER 16

Smoke Before Fire

Asha crouched behind a thicket of crinwood, fingers stained with berry juice, her youngest brother tangled in her braid like a vine with legs. The crinwood scratched at her calves, its bark flaking like old secrets, and the air smelled of damp moss and distant smoke.

She'd been tasked with steering her siblings away from the visitors, less diplomacy than containment, but her attention had splintered. She felt the weight of her mother's trust like a stone in her chest. Was she protector or jailer? Did the visitors bring danger or change? Her thoughts tangled like her braid, knotted with questions she couldn't yet name.

Her attention drifted away from the squealing chaos clambering over her knees.

Toward him.

She didn't know, at first, what made her look.

The visitors had been arriving all morning, a steady trickle of unfamiliar faces and foreign cloth, and she had watched them with the same guarded curiosity she gave to any strangers. But something about this one snagged her attention like a fishhook catching flesh, sharp and sudden and impossible to ignore.

He stood apart from the others, wrapped in reedcloth that whispered of distant water, its weave finer than anything made in her village. The late afternoon light fell across him in a way that seemed almost deliberate, gilding the edges of his dark hair, catching in the folds of his cloak. His skin was smooth and pale, lacking the weathering of hers and her kin's, whose earth-toned bodies wore the sun and wind like second skin. His brow sloped differently, his jaw finer, his mouth resting in something that looked like uncertainty, or perhaps simply patience.

No bone charms hung at his throat. No heavy tools weighed down his belt. No scar-wisdom marked his forearms, those badges of hunts survived and lessons learned in blood. Just hands, she noticed, watching the way his fingers moved as he sorted through his pack. Delicate hands. Hands that looked like they'd learned more from listening than from labor, more from holding still than from striking.

Something shifted in her chest. A loosening, or

perhaps a tightening. She couldn't tell which.

She tilted her head without meaning to, and berry juice tracked down her wrist like a thought interrupted, cool and sticky against her skin. Her brother squirmed against her side, demanding attention she could not give him.

The men she knew laughed from the belly. They stamped when they spoke, slapped backs, argued like rain breaking open stone. Their presence was tactile, strong and unapologetic and familiar as her own heartbeat. She had grown up measuring herself against that kind of man, wondering which one she might someday choose, which one might stand beside her mother without shrinking.

This one was nothing like them.

He moved like smoke before fire. Quiet. Attentive. Out of place in a way that should have made her dismiss him, should have made her turn back to her brothers and her duty and the familiar weight of her mother's expectations.

Instead, she watched. She watched the way he paused to study the bone archways with genuine wonder in his face. She watched the careful way he set down his pack, as though even his belongings deserved gentleness. She watched his stillness, which was not the stillness of weakness or fear but something else entirely, something that reminded her of deep water, of currents that moved beneath the surface where you couldn't see them.

Her mother's voice echoed in her memory: "Choosing isn't about liking someone. It's about who you want beside you when the winter stars scream and no one sleeps."

She didn't know this stranger. Didn't know his name or his people or whether he could survive a single night on the tundra without freezing. And yet.

"That one," she murmured, barely louder than breath. The words escaped before she could stop them, rising from somewhere deeper than thought. "He doesn't belong here."

Her brother looked up at her, confused.

She swallowed. Her heart had begun to beat differently, faster and somehow louder, as if it had suddenly remembered it existed. "I hope he stays anyway."

As if he'd heard her, though the distance was too great, he turned.

His gaze swept across the village, across the bone huts and the cooking fires and the children darting between adults' legs. It passed over the thicket where she crouched, and for one endless moment, it seemed to catch on her.

Not directly. Not boldly, the way the village boys looked at her, with challenge or hunger or the need to be seen looking. This was different. His gaze grazed past her like a question he wasn't sure he was allowed to ask, like someone who'd felt themselves named in a language they didn't quite speak.

The world contracted to that single point of almost-contact. The noise of the village, her brother's squirming, the scratch of crimwood against her calves, all of it faded to a distant hum. There was only the space between them, charged with something she couldn't name, and his eyes, dark and uncertain and somehow already familiar.

Then he looked away, and the world rushed back in.

Asha smiled, startled by the warmth spreading through her chest. And then she snapped too loudly at her brothers, because her heart was fluttering like a stunned bird and she didn't trust the sound it might make if left unguarded.

Her mother's warning clung like ash: "Trade before talk. Talk before trust. Trust only the river."

Still, Asha lingered near the edge of the village, pretending her feet had wandered of their own accord. She watched them unwrap their camp, knot unfamiliar fibers, murmur in half-formed rhythms that sounded like water learning to speak. The air was thick with the scent of fish-ink, firewood, and something foreign, like salt from a sea she'd never seen.

Then her brother, tiny and opinionated and utterly without restraint, burst through the fog of her watching.

Straight to the one crouching near a bag of tusk rings.

N'Kai.

Asha chased after, heart pounding from how the stranger looked up with no startle, no scowl. Just a quiet curve in his face, waiting. Patient. As if her brother's intrusion was not an interruption but an arrival.

"Why do your eyes sleep wrong?" the boy asked in the trade tongue.

N'Kai blinked, his fingers pausing mid-knot.

"They are not tired. Only slanted," he said carefully. "It is how my family folds vision."

The boy frowned.

"Like bark?"

"No, no, like..." N'Kai tried again, flustered, his hands fluttering like startled birds. "Shadow hats?"

Asha stifled a snort.

"Your smell is of old wind and fish-ink."

"That is very true. We fish. We ink."

"And your words dance badly."

"They trip often, yes."

Asha reached them, scooping her brother into a half-tackle. Her braid slipped over N'Kai's hand, the contact accidental or not, she wasn't sure. His skin was warm. She noticed that. She noticed too much.

"Sorry," she muttered. "He practices language without mercy."

N'Kai rose solemnly, brushing dust from his knees.

"His speech dances better than mine."

The boy wiggled loose and pointed at Asha.

"She speaks like fur and bone soup. Thick!"

N'Kai tilted his head.

"Soup speaks?"

Asha grinned.

"He means I'm loud. Or rich. Or edible. Unclear."

Then the boy turned to N'Kai again, suddenly inspired.

"Do you like her?"

"Like?" N'Kai said, puzzled. "Do I... eat her?"

Asha gasped, half laughing.

"He means like in the... fond way. The wanting way."

N'Kai flushed, the color rising to his cheeks like dawn creeping across snow.

"I am still very hungry, apparently."

The boy giggled. Asha rolled her eyes.

"Now he thinks you proposed."

"I did not! Not unless stew is involved."

Asha shrugged playfully.

"We have stew. But it's thick and full of bone teeth."

"Perfect," N'Kai replied. "I like my mistakes chewy."

And somehow, with the child still wedged between them, the air felt warmer. The language failed, fumbled, misfired, and still made space.

Connection, even without clarity.

Asha glanced at N'Kai one last time before her brother tugged her away. She thought of smoke, of the way it rose before fire caught, carrying the promise of warmth before the flame itself appeared. She wondered what kind of fire he carried beneath all that quiet. And whether it would burn or warm.

She didn't know yet.

But she wanted to.

CHAPTER 17

The Gift

N'Kai carved the tooth in silence, crouched behind the flat stone where the wind couldn't find him. The bone was cool against his palm, dense and slightly porous where the root had once anchored it to the river bear's jaw. He had rubbed it with rendered fat that morning, softening the surface until it gave beneath his thumbnail, and now the tooth carried the faint mineral smell of old bone mixed with the greasy sweetness of tallow.

The fishbone knife slipped often, nicking his thumb again and again. Each cut stung sharp and immediate, then faded to a dull throb that pulsed with his heartbeat. Blood welled in thin lines across his knuckles, and he wiped them absently on his tunic, leaving dark smears that dried to rust. The knife itself was worn smooth from use, its edge honed thin as a reed's edge, and it made a soft scraping sound each time he drew it across the tooth—a whisper of bone meeting bone, intimate and ancient.

He worked the spiral slowly, following the curve the way water follows a channel. The shavings curled away in pale ribbons that fell to the stone and caught the light, translucent as fish scales. Bone dust gathered in the creases of his palms, gritty and fine, working its way beneath his nails and into the whorls of his fingerprints. When he paused to blow the dust away, it tasted faintly of chalk and something older, something that had once been alive and breathing and warm.

The afternoon sun pressed against his back, and sweat dampened the hair at his temples despite the wind's chill. His shoulders ached from hunching over the small work, and his eyes burned from the concentration. But he didn't stop. He wasn't sure what the gift meant yet—only that it had to be given.

He'd chosen the tooth from the river bear's jaw himself, after the elders had finished their rites. It was the smallest, slightly cracked near the base where some long-ago impact had left its mark, but its spiral echoed the curve of Asha's braid when she turned her head. The crack gave it character, he thought—a history written in bone, a story of survival. He'd kept it hidden for three days, waiting for the right moment. Or maybe just waiting for courage.

The spiral deepened under his knife, each pass revealing fresh bone beneath the weathered surface—pale cream giving way to ivory, the grain tight and fine as old wood. He traced the line with his thumb, feeling the groove catch against his skin, and something in him settled. The imperfection was part of it now. The blood he'd left in the carving, the hours of patient work, the way his hands had learned the shape of something meant for someone else.

That morning, he wrapped it in a strip of barkcloth and walked the long path to the weaving shelter. The air was thick with wet cedar and fermenting plum. He rehearsed what he might say, then forgot it all when he saw her.

Asha was crouched beside the dye pots, her fingers stained with elderberry and ash. She looked up, curious and unguarded, and he reached for the pouch at his belt.

"I brought you something," he said, voice rough.

She didn't answer right away. Just watched as he unwrapped the cloth and placed the carved tooth in her palm.

N'Kai didn't expect her to smile like that—wide, unguarded, the kind of smile that made the carved tooth in his hand feel suddenly sacred. He'd meant it as a gesture, a maybe, a half-formed offering. But now it felt like a beginning.

Asha reached for the tooth before he could speak, her fingers brushing his with a softness that made the air between them shift. She turned it over in her palm, tracing the uneven spiral with her thumb.

"It's listening," she murmured. "Even if it's a little dizzy."

He laughed—awkward, too loud—and rubbed the back of his neck.

"I carved it with a fishbone knife. It kept slipping."

"That explains the wobble," she said, still smiling. "But it's beautiful. It's trying."

She tucked the tooth into the pouch at her hip like it belonged there. Then she stood, brushing moss from her knees, and looked at him with that same quiet certainty.

"Come with me," she said. "The river's split is soft today. The roots give more when the water listens."

He hesitated, then nodded, falling into step beside her. The path was damp and fragrant—mint, elder, rain rot. Her braid swung as she walked, catching the light like a thread pulled from dusk.

From the weaving shelter behind them, her parents watched. Her mother's hands paused mid-weave. Her father's gaze lingered, unreadable though not unkind.

"They're watching," N'Kai muttered.

"They always do," Asha replied. "It's how they know when to pretend they weren't."

She handed him a digging stick, worn smooth from use.

"You're going to ruin your tunic," she said.

"I already did," he said, showing her the carving dust still clinging to his sleeve.

She laughed, and the sound curled through the reeds like a half-remembered hush song.

CHAPTER 18

Bone-Dodge

Ash hung in the air like breath held too long.

The bone struck dust and silence.

N'Kai stood just inside the ash circle, breath steady, eyes on the bone. Meko wiped blood from his lip—his own, earned. Bran stretched his shoulder, wincing. The game had ended without a winner, but not without a shift.

Asha hadn't moved. Her gaze lingered on N'Kai a moment too long. She wondered if he dodged because he feared being chosen—or because he knew he already had been.

The boys gathered near the fire pit, where the bone now rested like a relic. No one spoke at first.

Bran broke the silence. He didn't look at N'Kai—he looked through him.

"Shadow-foot." He spat the words like gristle.

"Can't hit what won't stand still."

N'Kai didn't flinch. He felt the weight of Asha's gaze like a second heartbeat.

"I don't lie with my feet."

Meko chuckled, a sound like water finding its way around stones. "Ah, but consider—the feet are the only honest limb. The tongue flatters, the hands deceive, the eyes perform their little dramas. But the feet?" He spread his fingers wide, as if releasing something into the air. "The feet confess which direction the soul wants to flee. They are, in their way, prophets."

Bran tossed a pebble into the pit. It struck hard.

"She watched you."

"She watches everything," N'Kai said.

Meko leaned back on his elbows, his gaze drifting upward as though consulting the clouds for wisdom. "Not everything, sadly. When I split the ash with that magnificent throw—truly, the arc alone deserved a song—her attention had already wandered to quieter shores." He sighed with theatrical weight. "The ancestors saw. They wept for my unwitnessed glory. I felt their tears on the wind."

"She saw." Bran's jaw tightened. "Didn't care."

The silence that followed wasn't cruel. Just

honest.

Then Asha stepped forward, braid swinging like a blade. Her boot scraped the ash with a whisper.

"You boys throw bones like you're trying to impress the ancestors," she said, voice light but sharp. "They're dead. I'm not."

Bran's grin came quick and hard, teeth showing.

"Impress you, then?"

Asha tilted her head. She saw the bruises, the breathlessness, the hunger behind their eyes.

"Bran, you roar like a storm but miss half your throws. Meko, you spin like a dancer but forget the rhythm. And N'Kai..."

She paused. N'Kai met her gaze. He felt the question in her silence.

"You dodge like you're afraid of being chosen."

Meko's laugh came out wrong—too thin, stripped of its usual velvet. Bran looked away, the muscle in his jaw working like he was chewing something he couldn't swallow.

N'Kai said nothing. He wondered if being chosen meant being seen.

Asha stepped into the ash circle, smearing it

with her boot.

"Next time, maybe I'll play. See if any of you can dodge me."

Bran squared his shoulders. "You'd throw?"

"I'd aim for the heart," she said.

She sat beside the fire, uninvited but inevitable.

Bran tried again, leaning forward, elbows on knees, voice dropping low.

"You watched him. The whole time. Him."

"I watched all of you," she said. "But only one of you moved like he meant it."

Meko pressed a hand to his chest, his voice lifting into a lilting sorrow. "And now she asks us to guess which one, as though we haven't already begun composing our own funeral songs. Asha, you are a sculptor of small devastations. You chisel away at us with such delicate cruelty." He examined the scrape along his forearm with exaggerated melancholy. "My body is already ruined. Must you ruin my hope as well?"

Asha smiled, slow and merciless.

"If you don't know, it wasn't you."

Bran made a sound—half groan, half growl, bitten off at the edges.

"Mad. She'll drive us all mad."

"Oh, we arrived at madness long ago," Meko murmured, but his eyes had gone still, watching N'Kai with sudden clarity. "She is simply the one kind enough to name it. Some fevers, after all, feel like health until someone holds a hand to your brow and tells you the truth."

N'Kai stayed quiet, watching the bone. He felt the fire's heat on his cheek, the ash's chill on his skin.

Asha plucked the bone from the dust and turned it in her hands.

"You boys play like you're trying to win me. I'm not a prize. I'm the game."

Bran barked a laugh—short, hollow, more reflex than humor. Meko's face flickered, the mask slipping for just a breath before settling back into its knowing lines. N'Kai blinked once, slowly.

Asha tossed the bone back into the pit.

"Next time, I throw first."

They sat like that for a while—three boys, bruised and breathless, and a girl who had already won.

The fire crackled. The ash circle faded in the

wind.

And somewhere beneath the dust, something had shifted.

CHAPTER 19

Cold River, Warm Laughter

The river ran fast and glassy with snowmelt that had threaded through mammoth lands before finding its way here. It hissed along the stones as if trying not to wake them, whispering and slapping in a chorus of cold teeth and silver breath. The air carried the sharp, clean scent of pine and meltwater that stung the inside of N'Kai's nose with each breath.

Asha and N'Kai had walked to the pool together, drawn by something older than intention, something that moved beneath words rather than by plan or promise.

N'Kai stood ankle-deep in the current, his tunic folded on the bank beside him. His breath misted in the cold air like smoke from a reluctant fire. He wasn't used to cold like this. Riverlow water was slow and warm, respectful of the body it touched. This river bit. It pressed icy fingers into his ribs and whispered warnings he could almost hear: turn back, turn back.

He didn't turn back. But he hesitated, his body tensing against the cold that climbed his calves.

Asha stood at the river's edge, watching the lowlander deliberate as though he were courting the water itself, weighing his approach like a hunter tracking prey.

"You bathe with ceremony," she called out, her voice bright with amusement. "Is the water waiting for a speech?"

N'Kai startled at her words, then exhaled a small laugh. He rubbed his arms, trying to coax warmth back into his skin. "I was preparing," he said.

"For what?" she laughed, the sound carrying across the water. "A frost kiss?"

He opened his mouth to respond, then closed it again, the words tangling somewhere between his thoughts and his tongue.

Before he could find his answer, Asha kicked off her wraps and waded in. She splashed high, arms swinging like reeds caught in rebellion, her movements bold and unrestrained. The cold hit her like a dare, but she was used to it. Born in it. Her bones sang in the chill as though the ice itself were a familiar song.

She slapped water toward him without mercy, sending spray arcing through the air.

"This is how you enter a river," she shouted, her eyes gleaming with challenge. "As prey, not as a priest!"

He tried to dodge, to protest, but her grin was too wide and too wild to resist. She waded closer, the water churning around her thighs.

Then she placed both hands on his shoulders, her grip firm and certain. "Let the ice teach you," she said.

And she ducked him.

The water was agony. Brief and total. It roared across his scalp, filled his ears, invaded every hollow of his body with shocking cold that stole his breath and scattered his thoughts. The world became nothing but frigid pressure and the muffled thunder of the current.

He surfaced, gasping. The river clung to him, cold and insistent, water streaming from his hair and running in rivulets down his face. He blinked hard, his breath coming ragged, his heart thudding against his ribs like a trapped bird.

And then something broke loose inside him. Laughter. Bright and involuntary, it cracked through him like ice giving way to thaw. He wiped his eyes with shaking hands, his face glowing with sudden warmth despite the cold, his whole body alive with sensation.

"Again," he gasped, the word tumbling out before he could think.

Asha stared at him, her hair slicked back from her face, lips parted in surprise, eyes narrowed with something that looked like joy but ran deeper. "Then you are mine," she said softly, the words meant mostly for herself but carried to him on the cold air.

He looked at her across the small distance of water between them and felt something shift inside his chest. The cold no longer bit at his skin. It welcomed him, embraced him, made him part of the river itself.

The current rushed past them both, indifferent to the moment unfolding in its flow, but carrying it forward nonetheless.

CHAPTER 20

Asha's Choosing

By dusk, the wind whispered through the bone huts like a curious grandparent, its icy breath stirring the rich aroma of stew and mingling with the earthy scents of bark and wood. The sky spilled silver across the mammoth ridge, and everything in camp moved a little slower, as though even the shadows were listening.

Asha stood just outside the fire ring, her braid looped twice, her pouch bouncing against her hip with every impatient sway. She had plum seeds in her pocket and bark paper tucked into her boot. She was ready.

Her mother stirred the stew like it had offended her. Her father carved in quiet, letting the vertebrae speak first.

"I'm choosing," Asha said, placing the words carefully, like beads on a line. Clear, neither loud nor whispered.

Her mother paused for one breath, then resumed stirring. "Of course you are."

Asha stepped closer, bouncing once on her toes. "I'm choosing him. The riverlands man."

Her father looked up from the bone he'd been scoring, his eyes steady. "Does he know?"

"Not yet," Asha said. "But I do."

She thought of the way N'Kai listened—with his whole posture, not just his ears—like he was trying to memorize the shape of her silences. She remembered the time he helped her gather plum seeds after a storm scattered them across the ridge, how he'd tucked one behind her ear and said it was a promise.

Her mother snorted softly. "If he runs, I'll claim his boots."

"He won't," Asha said, grinning. "They're tied too tight."

Her mother pulled the seal-hide wrap tighter around her shoulders. She didn't sit. When she spoke, her voice carried the weight of something old.

"You're not the first of us to choose from the riverlands."

Asha had expected this. She planted her feet

and waited.

"Venari chose a riverlands man. Soft-handed. Knew the names of flowers." Her mother's voice flattened. "He never learned to build. Said he didn't need walls, that love would teach him. She believed him."

Asha watched her mother's hands move through the stew, stirring memories along with root and bone.

"He brought her bark that snapped in the fire. Didn't know seal sinew from weed-thread. She died three winters later—of waiting, not cold." Her mother looked up, eyes hard. "When you choose from far off, you bring more than a man. You bring his winters. His hunger. And if you're not careful, it's you who starves."

The silence stretched between them. The fire crackled and settled.

Asha let the story land. She felt its weight, acknowledged its warning. Then she straightened her shoulders.

"N'Kai isn't that man."

"You sound certain."

"I am." Asha's voice didn't waver. "He's already learned to read bone-grain. He asks before he assumes. He doesn't promise walls—he builds them, and he listens to Father while he does it." She met her mother's gaze directly. "Venari's man wanted to be loved. N'Kai wants to belong. There's a difference."

Her mother studied her for a long moment. Something shifted in her expression—not softening exactly, but settling, like snow finding its final shape after the wind dies.

"You've thought about this."

"I've done nothing but think about it." Asha allowed herself a small smile. "Well. Think about it and watch him fail at bone-dodge."

Her father set down his carving. The sound was quiet, deliberate.

"Then it's time." He didn't say time for what, but the meaning settled like moss over stone. Time to speak to Ma'ren. Time to offer the trade. Time to begin the kind of waiting that reshapes futures.

"I'll offer him the trade," he said.

Her mother blinked. "You'll—what?"

"I'll offer him the trade."

Taman didn't speak often, but when he did, the words settled like stone. He was the master builder of the Bone Vault, the great shelter that curved like a mammoth's ribcage against the northern wind. Every arch, every joint, every binding of sinew and ash was his. The elders said he could read the memory in bone—where it bent, where it broke, what it bore.

Many had asked to apprentice under him. Hunters, weavers, even the chief's own son. But Taman had refused them all.

"He may be good with fire and fiber," Taman said. "Let's see if he can shape shelter from what remains."

It wasn't just generosity. It was naming N'Kai as someone worthy of legacy—accepted rather than merely tolerated.

Her mother sighed, but the sound carried warmth beneath its weariness. "You always do things sideways, Asha."

"I get there eventually." Asha bounced on her toes again, energy crackling through her like summer lightning. "Just with flair."

She turned from the firelight before her parents could see how wide her smile had grown. Her pouch was full of plum seeds, her heart full of almost. The wind carried her forward, and she let it, walking toward the riverlands camp where N'Kai waited without knowing he was waiting.

Later, her parents walked together toward

Ma'ren's tent. Elen wore her seal-stiff robes, and Taman carried bonework slung over his shoulder. No announcement. No drums. Just the deliberate rhythm of offering.

N'Kai did not know yet.

But Asha did. She had always known—had known since the river, since the cold water and the way he'd gasped and laughed and asked for more. She had simply been waiting for the rest of the world to catch up.

The wind curled around her as she walked, and if it carried the ghost of Venari's sorrow, Asha acknowledged it with a nod and kept moving. Some warnings were meant to make you cautious. Others were meant to make you sure.

She had never been more sure of anything.

CHAPTER 21

Riverbend, Plum-Soup, and Choosing

The river glowed pale blue as it wound past the bone huts, slow and secretive. It whispered against the reeds, a hush-song of old secrets. Frogs croaked softly, then fell silent as if listening. The air was damp and cool, tinged with brine and the faint sweetness of plum.

Asha had set her pot just at the bend, where reeds tangled like old stories and frogs whispered judgment if you got too close. She crouched low, her braid swinging, her fingers stained from dye roots and river clay. Her eyes flicked toward the path, unreadable.

N'Kai approached with damp boots and a heart louder than he liked. He paused at the edge of the clearing, watching her stir the stew. Her shoulders were tense, her braid teased by the wind. She wore a single bear tooth at her throat, the one he'd carved poorly but gifted boldly.

"You came late," she said without turning.

He stepped closer, uncertain. "You didn't say when. I thought you meant dusk."

"I did. You just didn't understand the phrasing."

She ladled stew into a shell bowl and passed it to him. He hesitated. It smelled of plum seed, brine, and the mineral bite of river clay. The steam curled upward, catching the last light.

"What is this?" he asked.

"My choosing," she said. "You'll need to chew it carefully."

He stared at her, confused. The frogs had gone quiet. The wind shifted, brushing his cheek like a warning. She smiled, but her eyes held a weight he hadn't seen before—certainty braided with vulnerability.

"And also, you smell like burnt lichen. That's not part of the choosing. I just wanted to say it."

He laughed once, sharp and surprised, but the sound felt too loud. "Wait. Your choosing?"

She leaned on her elbows, eyes glittering. "You're slow, but warm. Like a stew left too long near the fire. I chose you days ago."

He swallowed a mouthful and nearly choked.

The stew burned at the back of his throat, but it was good, layered and intentional.

"Did anyone tell me?"

"No," she chirped. "That would've ruined the suspense."

He blinked. The silence pressed in. He looked at her again—braid messy, hands stained, grin like a tide about to tip the world over.

"I want this," he said slowly. "I want the way you speak like wind through reeds. I want the tooth you wear and the frogs that judge us. I want your tribe, your chaos, your stew, and the way you never wait for permission."

She leaned in, mock-serious. "Even the stew?"

He touched the rim of the bowl, then her wrist. "Especially the stew. It tastes like you meant it."

She grinned and tossed a sprig of rivermint into his bowl. "Then you're mine. But I'll still insult you daily. For balance."

They ate together, their laughter mingling with the mist that pulled thick over the bend. The frogs approved quietly. The river, never one for commentary, held the moment like it might remember it for years. The choosing settled between them like a stone finding its place in the current—weighty, deliberate, and wholly theirs.

CHAPTER 22

River Roots, Bone-Forked Paths

Ma'ren sat cross-legged on a seal-hide mat, her hands resting on the bone-rolls Asha's father had left. The edges curled like dried kelp, resisting permanence even here, inside the traveling tent they'd carried from the riverlands and pitched low against the tundra wind.

The tent was stitched from braided reedcloth and fish-leather, dyed in spirals of plum ash and ochre. It smelled of brine, smoke, and the memory of wet stone. The walls whispered when the wind pressed against them, like reeds remembering the current. The floor beneath them was soft with layered hides, and the air held a damp chill that clung to their skin like breath from the river.

Outside, trade murmured. Sleds creaked, dogs yawned and shuffled, voices bartered in clipped syllables. The scent of smoked fish mingled with foreign oils and the tang of iron tools.

The tundra light stretched long and pale, casting shadows across the snow-packed ground. On the horizon, a storm had begun to gather, its clouds bruised with violet and gray.

Inside, it was quiet.

She didn't look up when she said, "You know why I'm here."

He stepped through the flap, brushing past a curtain of antler beads. The air inside was warmer than outside, but still held the bite of tundra wind. He knelt beside her, close but not touching. His boots left damp prints on the mat, and his breath still steamed faintly. His shoulders were tense, his hands curled into his lap.

"I do," he murmured.

Ma'ren nodded, finally turning her gaze to him. Her eyes held sea-gray storms, unmoving but full of motion. She had once walked the choosing path herself, long before N'Kai was born. Her voice had sung the river's chant, and her name had been carved into driftwood and carried downstream.

"They've offered you place, trade, future. A name rooted here."

He stared at the scroll. "It's generous."

"And real," she said. "Something beyond guest-kindness or ceremony."

A gust rattled the tent poles. Somewhere outside, a trader laughed. A child called out in a language he was only beginning to understand. A drumbeat began, soft and steady, like a heart learning a new rhythm.

"I didn't expect it," N'Kai said. "I didn't think I'd want it." He shifted, his fingers tightening around his knee. "I thought I'd feel torn. But I don't. I feel drawn."

Ma'ren's voice gentled. "You do."

He pressed his fingers against his knee. The bone beads around his wrist trembled. One was cracked. He'd carved it too thin but refused to replace it. It had become a kind of truth.

"I love you. I love our ways. The chants. The tides. But when I stand with them, I don't ache to leave."

"You were born with wide sight," Ma'ren whispered. "I knew it the first time you pointed to sky-paths and asked where stars learned their names."

He blinked fast. "If I stay, am I breaking us?"

"No," she said. "You are stretching us. My voice in you will travel farther than I ever could."

She reached out, brushing his wrist. Her fingers lingered on the cracked bead.

"Grieve what you lose. Honor what you gain. That is how we stay true."

He nodded but didn't speak. Outside, the wind rose and fell in a long exhale. The drumbeat continued, steady and low. The storm had crept closer while they talked, its shadow darkening the tent walls.

Ma'ren leaned back, letting her hands rest again on the scrolls. "Tomorrow, you'll walk the choosing path. Someone who carries two tides, neither guest nor child."

He looked at her then, really looked. His breath caught, and he felt the weight of both worlds settle into his bones. "I'll carry you."

She smiled, faint and fierce. "You already do."

They sat in silence, the kind that didn't ask to be filled. The tent breathed around them, river-woven and wind-worn, holding the hush like a bowl. Outside, trade continued. Inside, something older was being exchanged.

The tundra, vast and listening, held space for both names and for the path between them.

CHAPTER 23

Feather and Farewell

The frost had lifted just enough to reveal the path stretching southward from the village. Six travelers stood at its edge, wrapped in cloaks woven from river-thread and weighed down with trade goods. They carried their burdens across shoulders or balanced baskets against their hips. No pack animals accompanied them, no sledges or wheels—only the steady rhythm of footfall and breath that marked those who traveled with purpose.

Ma'ren stood among them, her bearing unmistakably that of a Riverlands Elder. Every line of her posture spoke of dignity earned through years of leadership. Her pack sat secure across her shoulders, and her hair was braided in the traditional style of her people: three cords for lineage, one for loss, one for choosing. She conversed quietly with the caravan leader, her voice low and her gestures economical. She did not turn to look back at the village or at her son.

N'Kai remained beside Asha near the bone-arched gateway, his fingers repeatedly finding the carved feather she had given him days earlier. He watched his mother's careful movements, the way she held herself apart even while standing among the other travelers. The distance between them felt both necessary and unbearable.

Asha's mother arrived first, her arms laden with wrapped bundles. Despite the solemnity of the moment, warmth radiated from her as she pressed packages into Ma'ren's hands.

"You'll need the dried root for the crossing," Elen said. "And take the fireleaf. It burns hot and makes a racket, but it'll keep you warm through the worst nights."

Ma'ren received the offerings with the quiet grace that characterized all her movements. She bowed—with enough weight to acknowledge both the gift and the giver, though not deeply.

Taman approached next, carrying a flask of bark tea steeped in the traditional way. He offered it to Ma'ren along with a nod that conveyed more than lengthy speeches ever could.

"For the cold nights," he said. "And for the ones that seem warm but still need something to chase the chill from your bones."

Then Asha stepped forward. She held something wrapped in duskcloth, the fabric gathered carefully around its contents. "I carved this last night," she said, unwrapping it slowly. "It's a feather made from driftwood. I wove hair from both me and N'Kai into the shaft."

Ma'ren took the feather and studied it in the pale morning light. The carving was smooth and deliberate, etched with three symbols: one representing departure, one for the bonds that transcend distance, and one for the process of becoming. The woven hair was braided so tightly that the dark and light strands became inseparable, intertwining like currents where two rivers meet.

"You already gave one to N'Kai," Ma'ren observed.

"His is for staying," Asha said. "Yours is for carrying what stays with you even when you leave."

Ma'ren pressed the feather to her chest, just above her heart. When she spoke, her voice carried a rare note of emotion. "You understand more than you choose to speak aloud."

"I speak what needs speaking," Asha replied.

N'Kai finally moved closer, his eyes fixed on the feather in his mother's hands. "Will you keep it with your river stones?"

A small smile touched Ma'ren's lips. "No. I'll keep it with the bone tools where I can reach it when I work. It's sharper than any stone."

She turned fully toward him then, and for a moment she was simply his mother rather than the Elder of the Riverlands, seeing her son clearly. "You're staying. That's what you've chosen."

N'Kai swallowed hard against the tightness in his throat. "It hurts."

"It should," Ma'ren said. "But it's the right hurt. The kind that means you're growing toward something rather than away from it."

They embraced briefly but completely, standing bone-close with their breath held between them. Then Ma'ren released him and stepped back.

The caravan began to move. One by one, the travelers made their final adjustments—tightening pack straps, securing laces, settling their burdens more comfortably. Ma'ren joined the line without ceremony, her steps immediately falling into the measured cadence of those accustomed to long journeys. Her cloak trailed behind her like the edge of the river itself, catching the morning light.

They walked without formal farewell speeches or ritual gestures, yet every footfall carried the weight of parting. Each step took them further from the bone-built village and closer to the distant riverlands.

N'Kai, Asha, and her parents stood watching until the travelers disappeared into the shimmer of distance and morning haze. When the last figure finally vanished from view, Elen released a long breath.

"Well," she said loudly, breaking the reverent silence, "that was dignified enough to make the ancestors weep."

N'Kai blinked, pulled back from his thoughts. "She's always like that."

Elen's expression softened into a grin. "You'll miss her particular brand of quiet. But you'll learn to love the noise we make around here instead."

She reached up and ruffled his hair with familiar affection, then pulled him into a sideways embrace that squeezed the breath from his lungs. "Come on, river boy. Let's get some food into you before you start brooding like one of your mother's carved stones."

This time N'Kai didn't resist the comfort or the teasing. He let himself be drawn toward the warmth of the village.

Asha remained at the gateway a moment longer, her eyes on the empty southern path. She thought about Ma'ren's careful silence, her precise movements, the intricate braids that spoke of tradition and continuity. Then she glanced at her own mother—loud and generous, full of expansive gestures and easy laughter. Two women, two different rivers flowing through the world. Ma'ren carved from stillness and contemplation, Elen shaped by exuberance and flood.

Asha's fingers found the feather tucked into her belt, the twin to the one N'Kai carried. It served as both tether and promise—a reminder that what was carried in the heart could be kept even across great distances. She turned and followed N'Kai and her mother back into the village, back toward the shelter they were building together, back toward the life they were choosing.

Behind them, the path lay empty beneath the brightening sky, waiting for the next travelers, the next farewells, the next journey between worlds.

CHAPTER 24

Riverside Seduction

It wasn't the first time Asha had interrupted his work. But it was the first time N'Kai couldn't pretend to care.

She waited until his hands were full—lifting a curved bone, taut with sinew—as Asha's father watched with his usual silent approval. The tusk brace trembled in his grip, the weight uneven, the angle unforgiving. Sweat beaded at his brow, not from exertion, but from the nearness of her.

Then, like a shadow slipping through reedgrass, she crouched beside the water, grinned, and splashed.

The river caught the light—blue-gold, flickering like memory—and flung it toward him in droplets. It gurgled low, like a throat clearing before speech. The wind carried the scent of wet stone and plum skin. N'Kai cursed playfully, wiped his face, tried to ignore her. He knew the rules. The shelter wasn't finished. The choosing wasn't complete. The ache wasn't permission.

If he let her in now, the shelter might never rise. And without the shelter, the choosing would fail. And without the choosing...

Then came the whisper-soft fingers at his back. Just three. Just long enough for his breath to skip. Then gone again.

Asha darted to the far bank and lay back in the grass like she owned the sky. She lay back like someone who'd never been told no. Her braid fanned out behind her, catching bits of leaf and starlight. Her tunic was damp at the hem, her knees streaked with river mud. She hummed something tuneless and old.

N'Kai tried to return to the bonework. He lifted the brace again, adjusted the lashings, nodded when Asha's father grunted approval. But his hands shook. Not from strain. From proximity. Each time she laughed, the lashings slipped.

That night, the wind shifted. The river stilled. And the half-formed shelter beneath mammoth ribs held its breath.

N'Kai stirred from exhausted sleep to find her beside him—mud on her knees, stars in her braid, eyes gleaming.

She didn't speak at first. Just watched him, her head tilted slightly, as if waiting for the moment to catch up to itself.

"You build with bone," she said in a voice low and unstudied. Then, softer, "I build with joy."

He opened his mouth, but the words tangled behind his teeth.

She kissed him before he could answer.

And this time, N'Kai didn't resist. He didn't even think.

Her mouth was warm, insistent, tasting of plum and river salt. Her hands found his shoulders, his jaw, the cracked bead at his wrist. He pulled her closer—not out of hunger, but out of recognition.

Outside, the wind moved through the ribs of the shelter like breath through a flute.

Inside, they folded into each other—unfinished, unspoken, but certain.

The shelter was not yet complete.

But something else was.

They lay together in the hush, the mammoth bones arching above them like a promise. The moon hung crooked over the treeline, casting speckled light through the unfinished roof. The wind caught dried moss and lifted it like breath.

And the night, generous and wide, held them without judgment.

They lay close—Asha on her stomach, legs strong, playful grin flickering even in stillness. N'Kai was half-drunk on her—on her scent, her laughter, the way she'd whispered nonsense against his ear until he forgot the ache in his arms.

They touched not like strangers, and not like the claimed. They touched like people who had seen each other at the river and decided.

When they finally joined, it was messy, awkward, and radiant. Bone dust clung to their hands. The shelter creaked gently overhead. The mammoth ribs groaned like old memory, but held.

Outside, the river whispered its approval.

Later, wrapped in furs and the scent of each other, N'Kai whispered, "You make me forget everything that came before."

Asha just pressed her fingers to his lips.

CHAPTER 25

Dawnlight Consequence

Morning arrived gently, filtering through the gaps in the mammoth bone framework. N'Kai woke to warmth—layers of furs scattered around them, Asha curled against his side with her breath soft and steady against his shoulder. Beyond the shelter's entrance, frost was lifting from the pale curves of bone, and early mist crept between the structures like a carefully kept secret. The air carried the scent of damp earth mingled with woodsmoke from the village fires, and somewhere in the distance a bird called out with a low, fluting note that echoed through the valley.

He rose carefully, trying not to disturb Asha. His limbs ached from the previous day's building work and from the thousand small muscles that intimacy had awakened. His fingers bore smudges of ash and bone dust. Asha stirred at his movement, her eyes opening halfway. She didn't speak, but her gaze held laughter and knowing.

Mist curled along the river's edge with the soft texture of woven cloth. The mammoth ribs of their shelter glowed pale amber in the rising light, casting long shadows that seemed ceremonial in their stillness. Asha traced her fingers along the curve of N'Kai's collarbone as if memorizing something she hadn't yet fully experienced.

N'Kai watched her in silence, uncertain whether to break the quiet with words or to remain inside this hushed understanding between them.

Then came the sound of footsteps approaching —slow and deliberate, without any note of surprise.

Taman stood at the shelter's entrance, his silhouette framed by the sun's first reach across the landscape. He didn't speak immediately. His expression revealed neither anger nor amusement. He simply observed what lay before him: the unfinished lashings still waiting for attention, the two young people beneath the arching ribs, the evidence of their night together.

Then, with a single nod that conveyed neither explicit approval nor denial, he stepped forward into the shelter's interior.

"I see the bones hold," he said, his voice low and measured. "And the shelter stands."

Asha released a breath she hadn't realized she was holding. "He knew this would happen," she said quietly to N'Kai.

N'Kai nodded in agreement. "He knows everything that happens in this village."

They rose together, their movements slow and careful like the bones surrounding them. N'Kai reached for the coils of sinew, for the tusk brace waiting to be secured, for the work that still needed completion. This time his hands moved with steadiness rather than nervous uncertainty.

As N'Kai stepped outside into the fuller light, he found Taman positioned near the fire pit, sharpening a bone tool with deliberate strokes. The older man looked up, his gaze taking in the streak of bone dust across N'Kai's chest and the way his usually neat braid had come undone during the night. Taman nodded once—a simple acknowledgment that carried more weight than lengthy conversation.

No words passed between them. Only recognition.

But N'Kai felt the full weight of that silent exchange—the unspoken expectation that he would continue his work, the test that required no announcement to be understood. He bent to lift the next piece of tusk that needed positioning and carried it carefully to the shelter frame. The work continued through the morning, quieter than before and steadier, with something now rooted deep in the heartwood of shared memory and new commitment.

The shelter was no longer merely a task to be completed or a test to be passed. It had transformed into something more profound—a vow made visible, a promise given form through bone and sinew.

Asha didn't leave to attend to other duties. She remained beside him, threading fresh rivergrass through her braid while humming that same wordless melody she often carried with her. Her presence anchored the work, made it feel less like labor and more like ritual.

The shelter that had begun as a structure of survival and necessity was becoming something else entirely. With each lashing secured, with each joint properly fitted, it grew into a dwelling that would hold not just their bodies but their shared life together.

A beginning rather than simply an ending of his time as an outsider. A threshold crossed, a new story commenced.

CHAPTER 26

Legacy in Bone

By midday, the shelter stood complete.

The mammoth ribs arched overhead in graceful curves that suggested memory made solid. The sinew lashings held with the firmness of promises kept. Moss lined the inner walls, soft and fragrant, stitched together with panels of chantcloth and woven rivergrass. The interior smelled of earth and growing things, of careful work and intention.

Asha had woven a small braid into the upper beam—her own hair, dark and glossy, knotted together with sinew and salt-thread. Her fingers moved with reverence as she worked, each knot carrying unspoken meaning. She thought of her mother and the stories that had been braided into her childhood like threads through fabric. She thought of N'Kai, whose silences had gradually become as meaningful to her as any spoken words—a language of presence and attention.

N'Kai watched her work without speaking. He understood that this wasn't an act of possession or claiming. It was a marking, a way of saying that this place mattered, that what happened here would be remembered. He felt something press against his chest—not physical weight, but the pressure of significance. The shelter had become a vessel holding more than bone and moss. It contained the shape of their becoming, the transformation from separate individuals into something shared. He wondered whether it would hold them safely through the spring thaw and through all the long, quiet seasons that would follow.

Taman returned at dusk, carrying a bundle of smoked fish wrapped in hide and a single feather—black and curved, taken from a bird that nested only in the harsh conditions near the glacier's edge. The scent of the fish spread through the air, rich and briny, mingling with the earthier smells of moss and firewood smoke.

He placed the feather carefully at the shelter's threshold, positioning it as deliberately as if setting a foundation stone. Then he lowered himself to sit beside the fire. When he spoke, his words carried the weight of ritual and teaching.

"You built with bone," he said, looking at N'Kai. "She built with joy." His gaze shifted to Asha, then back to encompass them both. "Now build with memory. My mother once told me that a shelter's purpose isn't to keep the wind out—it's to keep the story in. You've braided your names into these ribs. Let them remember you. Let them hold what you're building together."

It was the first time Taman had addressed N'Kai with such directness, speaking to him not as an apprentice or outsider but as someone who belonged.

Asha's smile spread slowly across her face, quiet and deep. N'Kai bowed his head—not in submission or deference, but in genuine gratitude for the blessing being offered. He felt the fire's warmth against his skin and heard its crackle that sounded almost like breathing. His thoughts turned to the glacier bird that had given its feather, to the long migrations such creatures made, and to the way important stories could nest in silence and patience, growing stronger for being held close rather than spoken too soon.

That night they slept beneath the arched ribs once more. But this time the shelter had changed. Where before it had creaked and shifted as they moved, settling into its new form, now it rested easy. The joints held firm. The structure had found its balance.

The shelter breathed around them—not literally, but in the way that finished work seems to take on life of its own, becoming more than the sum of its materials. The bones remembered the mammoths they had been. The moss remembered the forest floor. The sinew remembered strength and flexibility. And now the shelter itself would remember the two people who had built it together, who had woven their lives into its frame.

Somewhere in the darkness beyond the fire's glow, the shelter dreamed its own dreams of holding and keeping, of witnessing and remembering, of being both protection and promise for whatever would come.

CHAPTER 27

One Year Later—Where the Bones Hold Warmth

The thaw arrived early that year, releasing the frost's grip on the bone huts and loosening the reserve that winter always brought to the villagers. A full year had passed since N'Kai first walked into this place—uncertain, largely silent, carrying riverland habits and an aching hunger for belonging that he hadn't fully understood until he found it.

The bone huts no longer appeared strange or foreign beneath his hands. He worked with natural rhythm now, understanding instinctively how a mammoth's spine must be angled to redirect wind, how incorporating salt-flower into the binding stitch could prevent the cold from penetrating too deeply. The elders observed his work with the particular quality of not-watching that signaled trust—they no longer needed to supervise because they knew he understood the craft.

His hands had learned the specific weight of bone, the way it resonated when shaped correctly. The sounds of his carving—soft scrapes of blade against surface, occasional sharp cracks as pieces separated—had become familiar music in the village. Some of the children had started humming along to the rhythm of his work.

Taman no longer hovered nearby during construction projects. Instead he passed tools in companionable silence, offered approving nods when N'Kai executed a particularly good joint, and once—only once—had referred to N'Kai as "my son" in the trade tongue, speaking just loud enough that Elen might overhear from where she worked nearby.

Elen had learned to read N'Kai's silences, responding to them with characteristic snorts of amusement, running commentary, and frequent refills of his stew bowl. She still offered casual insults, but they carried the particular affection reserved for family members who had proven themselves worthy of such familiarity.

The village had woven N'Kai into its fabric. Not as decoration or curiosity, not as a temporary guest or exotic addition, but as something fundamental—a root that had found purchase in new soil and was now part of what held everything together.

He noticed small signs of his integration everywhere. Some of the children had begun unconsciously mimicking his way of walking when they thought no one was watching. The bone carvers had adopted one of his riverland twisting techniques, incorporating it into their traditional methods. The plum seed stew now carried his preferred blend of spices, though Asha pretended not to notice when he commented on it.

Occasionally N'Kai still wondered whether he had truly earned his place here or whether some final test awaited him. But when he caught Asha watching him from across the communal fire—her braid half-loosened from the day's work, her eyes steady and knowing—he felt certainty settle in his chest like warmth spreading from a hearth.

In the evenings, he and Asha sat together beneath the ribs of their own shelter. The structure combined mammoth bone with driftwood, built through a process that had involved arguments and laughter and sudden moments of shared insight. She still teased him regularly, especially when he attempted to identify stars without consulting the proper bone-maps the elders used for navigation.

"You've become terribly useful," she said one evening, her fingers working at a stubborn knot in her braid while her eyes sparkled with humor. "We may have to keep you around just for kindling preparation and general chaos management."

N'Kai grinned and reached over to tug gently at her braid. "I stay for the insults. The excellent stew is merely a pleasant bonus."

Wind moved through the ribs of their shelter, creating a sound like a lullaby stitched together from driftwood and accumulated memory. N'Kai leaned back against the wall, listening to the quiet sounds of evening, to the bones that now held warmth instead of cold. He thought about the river where he had grown up, about the long walk northward with Ma'ren, about the first time he had laid hands on a mammoth spine and felt its potential for becoming shelter.

He didn't know what the future would bring or what shape his life would ultimately take. But he knew with certainty that he would carve it, stitch it, and live it fully—rooted in this place, ready for whatever came next.

CHAPTER 28

River Whispers and Soft Reveals

The quiet that surrounded the river held something sacred, as if the water itself had paused to listen to what would unfold on its banks.

The river ran still beneath the bone bridge, producing only the soft sound of water threading through reeds and the occasional thump of fish striking stone. The air hung damp and cool, carrying the scent of moss and the faint metallic tang of silt stirred by current.

N'Kai squatted by the bank, working at a fishing net that had developed several troublesome tangles. He muttered under his breath about stubborn knots and fish that seemed to hold personal grudges against him. Asha stood behind him, selecting smooth pebbles from the mud and tossing them into the water with deliberate aim and no apparent concern for disturbing his concentration.

"If you keep cursing at the net, the fish will hear you and swim to calmer waters," she said. Her voice carried its usual lightness, but something deeper ran beneath the teasing tone.

"I don't need them to like me," N'Kai replied without looking up. "I need them to sit still long enough to get caught."

Asha plucked another smooth stone from the mud, then crouched beside him. Instead of throwing this one into the water, she began drawing in the wet silt—a spiral that curved inward on itself in the traditional counting pattern.

"What's that for?" N'Kai asked, glancing over at her work.

"Counting spiral," she said, grinning, though her eyes shifted briefly toward the river as if seeking permission or acknowledgment from the water itself. "You've got one season to improve your net-mending skills before we'll need stew for three people instead of two."

The meaning of her words hit him with sudden force. The spiral stopped him completely. He dropped the net, forgetting the tangles he'd been working to free.

"Wait," he said slowly. "Stew for three? Are you saying—"

Asha leaned her head against his shoulder with apparent casualness, though her breath caught slightly as she settled against him.

"I told the river before I told you," she said. "It's kept the secret well enough. I figured you might react exactly like this—dropping whatever you were holding."

N'Kai stared at the spiral drawn in the silt, then at Asha's face, then back to the curved line of the counting pattern. His heart began pounding with the same insistent rhythm as fish striking stone.

"I might drop everything," he admitted. "Are you—are we—is this real?"

She took his hand and turned it palm-up, then placed the smooth stone she'd been holding into it, closing his fingers around the marker of what was beginning.

"It's already begun," she said simply.

N'Kai didn't speak for a long time. He sat holding the stone, his thumb tracing the spiral pattern again and again. His thoughts swirled like eddies in the current—images of tiny feet, of lullabies sung to the rhythm of the river, of nets cast for purposes that went far beyond catching fish. He thought of the shelter they had built together, and how it would soon hold more than just the two of them.

The river continued flowing past them, carrying their silence and transforming it into something sacred. The water seemed to acknowledge what had been spoken, bearing witness to the moment.

Asha closed her eyes, listening to the stillness that surrounded them. "It's a good place to begin," she whispered. "A good place for this to start."

N'Kai nodded, still unable to find words adequate to what he was feeling. But his grip on Asha's hand tightened, his fingers interlacing with hers.

The spiral stone rested in his palm, pulsing with all the possibility it represented. And the river, ancient and knowing, flowed on—offering what seemed very much like a blessing.

CHAPTER 29

The Naming Circle

They gathered at twilight in the ancient circle etched into the earth generations before anyone could remember. The old markings had been worn smooth by countless feet, yet they still held their power—this was sacred ground where names were received rather than given, where silence carried more weight than any spoken word.

No one knew who had first drawn the circle, only that those who entered must walk to the east, and that the center had to remain empty until someone chose to kneel.

Asha stepped forward into the gathering dusk. Her breath came steady and her palms hung open at her sides, though her heart hammered against her ribs with the rhythm of uncertainty. The others ringed the circle's edge and began to hum—not any melody she recognized, but a deep vibration that seemed to rise from the earth itself, low and resonant, as though the land were remembering its own name.

She moved slowly through the circle's perimeter. One hand traced a spiral pattern through the cooling air while the other pressed against her belly—not as performance but as acknowledgment of what grew there.

Across the circle, her eyes found N'Kai's. He stood motionless among the gathered villagers, but she felt something in him lean toward her despite the distance. His gaze held quiet hope and an unspoken question that hung between them like mist.

Asha knelt in the circle's center.

The humming softened around her, voices dropping to make space for what would come. The air thickened with approaching night and rising dust. Sage smoke drifted from the evening fires, mingling with the rich scent of turned soil.

She bent forward and pressed her lips to the earth, feeling its coolness against her mouth. Into the dark soil she whispered a name—so quietly that no one else could hear.

Not N'Kai watching from across the circle.

Not the villagers humming their bone-deep song.

Not even Elen, who had birthed seven children

and midwifed countless more.

Only the soil received the name, dark and patient and listening.

The name did not belong to Asha. It did not belong to N'Kai.

It belonged to the child who would come—the one already forming in the secret darkness of her body.

The name had arrived dream-born, carried to her in the stillness between one heartbeat and the next. Names were sacred things here, rooted in the unseen world that connected child to ancestor, breath to stone, present to past. They bound a person to their place in the great spiral of being.

This name would not be spoken aloud again until the child drew its first breath and opened its eyes to the world.

Asha rose without ceremony, brushing dust from her knees. Around her the humming resumed its former strength. The circle turned as villagers shifted their weight and breathed as one. The dust she had disturbed settled slowly back to earth, as if the ground itself were tucking the whispered name safely away.

N'Kai watched her stand, his chest swelling with quiet wonder he could barely contain.

Though no words had been spoken that he could hear, he understood that something fundamental had shifted in the silence. A beginning had been named and witnessed, even if no one yet knew what to call it.

The twilight deepened around them. The circle's ancient markings seemed to pulse faintly in the fading light, holding the secret that had been entrusted to the earth. Somewhere in the distance, a nightbird called. The wind carried the scent of smoke and sage across the gathered bodies.

Asha walked out of the circle and back to N'Kai's side. She took his hand without speaking. He squeezed her fingers gently, feeling the calluses on her palm from weaving and digging, the warmth of her skin against his.

The ceremony was complete. The name had been given to the earth for safekeeping until the child could claim it.

CHAPTER 30

Hush-Song

The light began to thin across the tundra—not fading but thinning, like breath drawn through woven cloth. The moon had begun its slow veiling of the sun, and with its passage came an unnatural stillness. The wind that had blown steadily all morning paused mid-gust. The river's constant murmur fell silent. Even the birds who had sung through grief and storm went quiet in the trees.

It was the hour of hush, when the eclipse neared its peak.

Inside the birthing shelter woven from river reeds and driftwood, the air grew heavy with waiting. Smoke from the small fire curled upward through gaps in the woven roof, carrying the scent of juniper and ashroot. The walls filtered the thinning light into soft shadows that moved across the packed earth floor.

Asha had been laboring since dawn, her body

straining through contractions that came closer and harder as the hours stretched on. She had begun with laughter that morning, teasing N'Kai about his worried face, making jokes with her mother and the midwife even as the first pains gripped her belly. Her eyes had sparkled with mischief then, her voice light and bright despite the discomfort. But as the sun climbed and the contractions deepened, her strength had slowly drained away. Now she lay barely conscious, curled against N'Kai's chest with her damp braid trailing across his arm. Her fingers tangled weakly in the folds of his tunic, holding on with what little grip remained.

N'Kai held her tightly, one arm supporting her shoulders while his other hand stroked her hair. He whispered comfort in her ear—words he barely heard himself, reassurances that felt hollow against the reality unfolding in his arms. His own heart thundered with a fear he could not name or control.

Elen knelt beside them on the shelter floor, one weathered hand resting on her daughter's ankle, the other pressed against her own mouth as if to hold back words or screams. Her mind swirled with memories she could not stop—Asha's first unsteady steps across the bone-paved yard, her stubborn refusal to wear proper boots in winter, her laughter echoing through the reeds when she and her brothers played their wild games.

The midwife crouched in the corner shadows, weeping soundlessly with her trembling hands pressed together.

The eclipse deepened outside. Light dimmed to a hush across the land. The world seemed to hold its breath. Colors faded from the vibrant hues of day into shades of ash and silver. The air inside the shelter grew noticeably cooler, tinged with the scent of river mist drifting in.

Then the child came.

Born in near-darkness, bathed in the eclipse's profound silence. There was no cry of entry into the world. No struggle or violent emergence. Just a slow unfolding, as if Asha's body remembered some ancient knowledge of how to open and release. The midwife leaned forward to receive the child—and stopped, her breath catching in her throat.

There was no blood.

Not a drop marked the child's skin. Not a trace stained the birthing cloths. The cord itself gleamed pale and clean, as if the birth had occurred somewhere outside the body's usual reckoning. The midwife had attended dozens of births, had seen easy ones and hard ones, had washed blood from her hands more times than she could count. But she had never seen this—a child delivered as if drawn from still water rather than flesh.

She crossed her fingers against ill fortune, then caught herself. This was not ill. It was simply other. Something the old stories hinted at but never fully explained.

With trembling hands she tied the cord with sinew thread and placed the child gently in the space between N'Kai and Asha.

N'Kai bent forward, pressing his forehead against Asha's. His tears traced the curve of her cheek and fell onto her shoulder. Asha's lips moved—not forming words but shaping melody. A hush-song rose from her, faint as dying breath but carrying a rhythm older than the village itself.

The song shaped itself in the space between her breath and the child's skin. Each syllable pressed into the newborn's tiny body with deliberate care. Asha's fingers, moving with the last of her strength, traced along the child's shoulder as if writing something invisible there. Her voice was barely audible above the silence, but the rhythm sank deep into the child's being.

She lifted her head slightly and whispered a name into N'Kai's ear—so quietly that only he could hear it. The name passed between them like a thread of light, intimate and sacred. Asha's final gift to him and to their daughter.

The child blinked, her eyes open from the very start, their gaze steady and knowing as the gathering dark. Around her tiny wrist, a lock of Asha's braid had somehow slipped loose and wrapped itself there like an intentional binding. The child's skin seemed to shimmer faintly in the eclipse light, as if dusted with silver ash from the shadowed sun.

Asha's breathing grew shallow. Her chest lifted once with effort, paused, lifted again more weakly, and then went still.

The shelter fell into absolute silence.

Elen reached forward and gathered the child into her trembling hands. She lifted the baby close to her chest but did not speak. None of them spoke. There were no words for what had just passed between the worlds.

Outside the shelter, the sun bowed fully beneath the moon's shadow. A perfect ring of fire crowned the darkened sky, casting an eerie orange glow across the bone huts and the frozen tundra beyond. The temperature dropped further. Frost began to form on the mammoth ribs that framed the shelter's entrance.

From somewhere in the shelter's woven roof, a single white feather drifted down—slow and deliberate in its descent, turning slightly as it fell. It landed gently beside Asha's open hand, its whiteness stark against her cooling skin.

Then, slowly, the light began to return to the world. The moon's shadow crept backward across the sun's face. Color seeped back into the land—first gray, then brown, then the pale blue of ice and sky.

Asha did not return with the light.

Her body remained still in N'Kai's arms, growing colder by the moment. But something of her breath seemed to linger in the shelter's hush, hanging in the air like smoke. And when the child drew her first full breath and released it in a tiny sigh, that exhalation carried the same rhythm as Asha's final song.

The hush-song had passed to the child—woven into her bone, threaded through her blood, embedded in the very memory of her cells. She carried her mother's voice in her skin, in the pattern of her breathing, in the way she would one day move through the world.

Outside, the eclipse released its hold. Light flooded back across the tundra. But inside the shelter, in the space between grief and birth, the hush remained.

CHAPTER 31

Frostline Walk

Grief did not arrive with sound. It settled like snow, quiet, uninvited, and absolute.

He did not bury her—that was not the way of her people. The dead belonged to bone and wind, not earth.

Her shelter stood solemn and still, built of mammoth ribs and fire-scorched tusk. Moss and hide wrapped the walls in memory. Asha lay within, blanketed in the same cloth that had once carried berry pulp, laughter, and fire warmth. The fabric still held faint traces of her scent: smoke and juniper, the sweet tang of crushed berries, the earthiness of worked leather. He had wrapped her himself, his fingers clumsy with shock, moving through the motions because his body remembered ritual even when his mind had gone blank.

Outside, the light bent strangely. It touched nothing directly but lingered on edges that did not need warming. It shimmered against the tusks, casting long shadows that reached toward the fire. The air held a peculiar stillness, as if the world itself was holding its breath, waiting for him to break.

He stood with a carved feather in one hand. Its sinew wrappings were frayed, worn from countless touches. A single strand of her hair had curled around it, caught by accident or fate. He could not remember when it had wound itself there, only that it had, and now he could not bear to remove it.

She had tied it to his tunic once, the morning after choosing him. Her fingers had been rough, deliberate, her touch both tender and possessive. "Now they'll know you're mine," she had said, her eyes bright with mischief and certainty. He had laughed then, had felt the weight of being chosen settle into his bones like warmth.

He placed the feather in her folded hands. Her fingers did not close around it, could not close around anything anymore. But he believed they might, given time. Given enough silence. Given a world where death could be undone by wanting it badly enough.

Smoke curled from the hearth, thick with mammoth oil, ritual, and the sharp bite of sacred herbs. The scent was overwhelming, pressing into his lungs until breathing felt like drowning. He did not cry, his tears having long since traveled downward, sinking into roots or stones or the dark earth beneath his feet. Perhaps into the child.

Their daughter slept near the fire, wrapped in Asha's shawl. The worn fabric rose and fell with her tiny breaths. Her cheeks were flushed with warmth and health, her small fists curled against her chest. She did not know grief yet. She knew only warmth, only the rhythm of breathing, only the muffled sounds of a world she had just entered. She would never know her mother's laugh, would never feel Asha's rough hands braiding her hair, would never hear the stories Asha would have told about mammoth hunts and berry-stained troublemaking.

Elen sat beside the child, her broad frame folded protectively around the sleeping infant. Elen, who had raised seven children of her own and midwifed countless more. Elen, who laughed too loud and loved too fiercely and whose expressive face now carried an unaccustomed stillness like a death mask. She did not speak. She only opened her arms when he looked at her, a silent invitation he could not accept. Her eyes lingered on Asha's form, and her breath caught once, just once, before she exhaled into silence. When she looked at him, her gaze held something he could not name. Pity, perhaps. Or recognition of a grief too vast for words.

He did not name the child, for some names arrived dream-born, whispered by mothers in their final moments. Asha had whispered one to him in those last hours, her eyes half-closed, her fingers tracing his throat like he was an instrument only she knew how to play. The name had been soft as breath, barely audible above her labored breathing. He had caught it, held it, treasured it. But he did not repeat it. It was not his to speak. It belonged to Asha and to the daughter she would never raise, and speaking it aloud felt like a theft he could not commit.

Names were more than sound here. They were memory, lineage, and promise woven together. To speak a name was to bind it to breath and bone, to call something into being and claim responsibility for its existence. He had no right. Not anymore. Not when he could barely remember his own name through the fog of grief.

Elen took the bundle gently, lifting the child with practiced ease. The fire sighed and settled. Wind pressed against the bone shelter, testing its edges, seeking entrance. The structure held, as Taman had built it to hold, as N'Kai had learned to build. Everything held except him.

A feather fell from above, soft as surrender, and landed in his boot. White and pristine, it rested there like an accusation. He could not bring himself to pick it up, could not bear to touch another feather, could not bear another reminder of flight or freedom or the lightness Asha had carried so effortlessly.

He turned. Stepped out into a world where everything had changed and nothing had. The tundra made no sound. Snow had not begun to fall, but the air tasted of it, sharp and metallic on his tongue. The sky hung low and gray, pregnant with storms that had not yet broken.

The frostline had started crawling. He could see it in the distance, a pale line advancing across the landscape like a slow tide. It moved like memory itself, slow and quiet and certain, erasing color and warmth as it came. Not a storm, but a boundary. A line between warmth and forgetting, between the world of the living and something else entirely.

He walked toward it. His feet moved without conscious thought, carrying him away from the bone shelter, away from the sleeping child, away from Elen's silent witness. He wore grief like a second skin, a layer that did not warm him but only wrapped him in heaviness. The cold bit at his exposed skin, but he barely felt it. Pain required presence, and he had already begun to absent himself from his own body.

The village fell away behind him. No one called

out. No one followed. They understood, perhaps, that some journeys must be taken alone, that some grief could not be shared or softened. The bone huts grew smaller, their curved ribs stark against the gray sky. The smoke from the fires became threads, then wisps, then nothing.

He walked until his feet bled inside his boots, until his breath came in ragged gasps that tore at his throat, until the cold had worked its way so deep into his bones that he could no longer remember what warmth felt like. The landscape around him slowly bleached of color. Green faded to gray. Brown dulled to ash. Even the sky seemed to lose its depth, becoming flat and featureless.

The frostline whispered to him as he walked. Not in words, but in feeling. A promise of rest. Of stillness. Of the kind of forgetting that came not from losing memory but from no longer caring whether memory existed at all. It offered him oblivion wrapped in ice, and he walked toward it with the single-minded focus of a man who had already decided.

Forget, the wind seemed to say. *Forget. Forget. Forget.*

And for the first time since Asha had died in his arms, he wanted to listen.

CHAPTER 32

The A'ta

Twilight fell like a hush over the frostline, bringing with it a silence so complete that N'Kai could hear the blood moving sluggishly through his veins. He had wandered long enough that hunger no longer spoke to him in the language of need. His body had moved past demanding food and now simply existed, each step a small miracle of continued motion. Only water still called to him, and he followed that call to a place where headwaters rose cold and silver-blue through rock seams. The same river he had once chosen, just as he had chosen her.

He knelt and drank without ritual, without pause, without the prayers his mother would have offered. The water burned his throat with cold, shocking his system briefly into alertness. It tasted of stone and distance, of places so high and remote that sunlight barely reached them. He cupped it in his palms and brought it to his lips again and again, drinking until his stomach cramped and his teeth ached.

The snow around him no longer whispered with wind. Even the river forgot its voice, flowing in eerie silence as if sound itself had been stripped from the world. His muscles ached with a deep, bone-seated pain that had become so constant he barely noticed it anymore. His feet had bled through his boots, leaving dark stains in the snow behind him. His breath made smoke that hung in the still air, refusing to dissipate.

Yet something stirred beneath the silence. A change in the quality of attention, as if the world had turned its gaze toward him. Not sound. Not shadow. Simply a shift in notice, the way prey animals sense a predator before seeing it.

He looked up and saw them. Not clearly at first, just the edges of their forms. Three figures stood at the boundary between twilight and full dark, their shapes difficult to hold in the eye. When he looked directly at them, they seemed to blur and shift. When he looked away, their outlines sharpened in his peripheral vision, becoming almost solid before dissolving again when he turned his head.

Their eyes were rimmed in something darker than dusk, a color like burnt memory or bruised moonlight. The darkness spread from their eyes like tears that had stained their faces permanently. Their mouths did not move, but he could feel their breathing, a rhythm that was wrong somehow, too slow or too fast or simply not aligned with the rhythm of living things.

Cloaks clung too closely to limbs not fully formed. The fabric, if it was fabric, moved with them as if part of their flesh rather than draped over it. Their forms shimmered faintly, neither pale nor warm, but touched by some unplaceable coolness that seemed to absorb light rather than reflect it. They cast no shadows despite the low sun, and the snow beneath their feet showed no imprint of their passing.

Their hands, when they reached toward him, were not cold or clawed as he might have expected. They were simply knowing, as if they had touched him before he was born and would touch him again after he died. Long fingers extended toward him, and he found he could not move, could not flee, could only kneel there in the snow and wait for what would come.

They moved with no weight, making no sound as they approached. Their motion had the quality of inevitability, like watching water flow downhill or watching night fall. There was no malice in their advance, no hunger that he could recognize as hunger. Only intent, pure and absolute.

The first figure reached his left wrist. Its fingers wrapped around him with a grip that was neither tight nor gentle but simply complete. The touch sent a shock through his system, and then warmth flooded him. Not the warmth of fire or sunlight, but something sweeter, more intoxicating.

Images flashed through his mind. His feet dancing across splitroot swings, the joy of movement without fear or thought. His mother sang in a language she had never taught him, words that felt ancient and comforting. Her face was softer than he remembered, gentler, all the hard edges worn smooth. He tasted berries he had never eaten, their sweetness exploding on his tongue. He saw memories that could not be his, moments too perfect to have ever existed.

The pleasure that tore through him was radiant, unbearable. It lit up every nerve ending, made his muscles clench and release in waves. He gasped, but not aloud. The sound died in his throat, trapped there like everything else. His childhood unraveled behind his eyes, the true memories dissolving and reforming into something beautiful and false. The hard winters became mild. The hunger became abundance. The loneliness became belonging.

And then it was gone. The first figure released him, and with its departure, his childhood went with it. He could no longer remember the feel of his mother's hand in his, could not recall the specific cadence of her voice when she sang the hush songs. The memories had been replaced by sweetness, by false comfort, by a lie that tasted better than truth ever had.

The second figure touched his right wrist before he could fully comprehend what had been taken. This time the extraction was more violent, more thorough. His manhood dissolved like morning mist pulled by wind.

The bone shelters vanished from his memory. Asha's father faded to a vague impression of size and warmth. Elen's laughter dispersed, leaving only an echo of sound without context. The whole year of building and learning and becoming part of the village simply unmade itself, the threads pulled loose until nothing remained but empty space where experience should have been.

In its place, he saw a life not his. He stood larger, louder, adored for things he had never done. Hands grasped tools he had never held. Lips kissed mouths he had never met. Voices cheered his name, but it was the wrong name, spoken by people who did not exist. He was a hero in battles he had never fought, a craftsman creating works he had never imagined, a lover skilled beyond anything he had actually experienced.

The sensation shimmered with sweetness that tasted like lies soaked in longing. It offered him everything he might have been if he had been braver, stronger, more worthy. The false memories felt more real than his actual life had ever felt, more vivid and complete. His fingers ached as if they had never steadied, as if the years of learning had been carved from someone else's story entirely.

Pleasure bloomed where belonging once lived, and he nearly wept. But the tears had nowhere to land. They evaporated before they could fall, stolen by the cold or by the figures or by whatever force governed this terrible exchange.

The third figure leaned close, and he knew what was coming. This would be the worst. This would take everything that mattered. He wanted to fight, wanted to run, but his body would not obey him. He was held not by force but by certainty, by the knowledge that resistance was meaningless.

Its breath grazed his throat, cool and oddly sweet. Not to puncture, not to feed on blood or flesh, but simply to retrieve what it had come for. When its fingers touched his chest, directly over his heart, he felt his entire being focus down to that single point of contact.

Asha began to unravel.

Her voice became wind, losing its particular timbre and cadence. The way she said his name, the slight catch in her breath before laughter, the particular tone she used when she was about to tease him. All of it scattered like seeds on the wind, impossible to gather back. Her smile fractured into snow, breaking apart into a thousand tiny pieces that melted before he could grasp them. Her laughter melted away like ice pressed to warmth, leaving only the memory of sound without the sound itself.

He forgot the curve of her brow, the exact placement of the small scar above her left eyebrow. He forgot the taste of her breath, which had always carried a hint of mint from the herbs she chewed. He forgot the berry-stained smile that arrived before her teasing, the way her lips curved more on one side than the other. The specific weight of her body against his in sleep, the sound of her breathing in the darkness, the way her hair had smelled of smoke and juniper.

Most painfully, he forgot the way she said his name like it belonged to her, like she had created it specifically for him. That particular inflection, that ownership, that certainty. It vanished completely, leaving only the generic sound of syllables without meaning.

The figure withdrew its hand, and with it went Asha. Not just the memory of her, but the shape her existence had carved into him. The space she had occupied in his heart simply closed over, as if she had never been there at all. He knew intellectually that something had been taken, could feel the absence like a missing tooth, but he could not remember what filled that space or why it mattered.

They left him kneeling in the snow as twilight deepened into full dark. There was no blood on the pristine white surface. No wound visible on his body. His wrists bore no marks. His chest showed no bruise. But he was empty in a way that went beyond hunger or grief.

He was unseen, even to himself. Whatever he had been before they touched him no longer existed. The vessel remained, but everything that had made it meaningful had been scooped out and carried away. He was hollow, a shell shaped like a man but containing nothing but echoes.

The three figures turned and walked back into the gathering darkness, and the twilight swallowed them as if they had never existed. The wind returned, tentatively at first, then with more confidence. The river remembered its voice and began to murmur again. The world resumed its normal patterns.

Only N'Kai remained changed. He knelt there as stars emerged overhead, as the temperature dropped further, as his breath continued to make clouds of vapor that dissipated into the night. He was alive but not living. Present but not here. A shape that had once contained a soul now held only hunger and emptiness and the vast, aching silence of everything he had lost without even the mercy of remembering what was gone.

CHAPTER 33

The First Dream

The First Dream came not as vision but as instinct, a shift in the fundamental nature of his being that required no explanation because it preceded thought itself.

He awakened beneath a sky the color of bone, bleached and ancient. The world had transformed while he knelt in the snow. Or perhaps he had transformed, and the world simply reflected back what he had become. He neither gasped nor blinked in surprise—he simply was, a shape carved from silence, a vessel waiting to be filled.

His body remembered how to stand, how to walk, how to move through space. But the why of movement had been stripped away along with everything else. He rose because rising was what bodies did. He walked because walking was the natural state of a thing with legs. Purpose had become irrelevant.

The snow beneath his feet did not resist his weight. It accepted him with the same indifference it showed to all things. Each step left a shallow impression that the wind immediately began to erase, as if even his passage through the world was meant to be temporary and forgotten.

He moved without direction, drawn by something he could not name because names themselves had lost their meaning. The landscape around him was vast and empty, stretching away in all directions without feature or variation. No trees broke the monotony. No rocks interrupted the smooth expanse of white. Just snow and sky and the space between them where he existed.

The First Dream was not a story or a narrative with beginning and end. It simply was. A state of being that had no opposite, no alternative. It was hunger without object, longing without target, the pure ache of absence given form and set walking across an empty world.

And though he did not know it, could not have articulated it even if language had still been available to him, the world had begun to remember him. Not as he had been, but as he was becoming. Something old and patient stirred in the deep places, taking note of this new emptiness walking across its surface.

Then he saw movement. A flicker of life beneath a frost-bitten root, small and urgent and utterly unlike the static emptiness of everything else. He turned toward it with the slow inevitability of water finding its level, drawn not by conscious choice but by the simple fact that movement called to stillness, that life called to the hollow place where life had been.

A squirrel crouched there, her body taut with the particular tension of a mother protecting young. Her fur bristled against the cold, each hair standing separate and distinct. She darted forward, then paused, her small body quivering with indecision. Then she returned to her nest, a hollow carved into the twisted roots of a long-dead tree.

Inside, three young slept in a tangle of warmth and breath, their tiny bodies pressed against each other for heat. They were impossibly small, impossibly vulnerable, their translucent eyelids showing the dark shadows of eyes beneath. Their whiskers twitched as they dreamed whatever dreams came to creatures so new to the world.

She curled around them with desperate grace, her body becoming a shield between her offspring and the killing cold. Her heartbeat was rapid, a drum of pure devotion that he could somehow hear despite the distance between them. She did not think of love in any way he would have recognized as thought. But she was love, embodied completely in the way only a mother could be, even in the smallest of forms.

Her memories rose from her like heat shimmer from sun-warmed stones. Simple things, uncomplicated by language or abstraction. The taste of pine nuts, sweet and rich with fat. The weight of her young when she first felt them move inside her. The rhythm of gathering before frost, the urgent need to prepare driving her to frantic activity. The fear of wings overhead, the shadow of hawks passing across the snow. The satisfaction of a full cache, the brief peace of knowing her children might survive another day.

He watched from a distance that felt both vast and infinitesimal. He could not have named her species or explained her behavior in any categorical sense. He only knew that she felt, and that her feelings rose from her with a brightness that called to the darkness inside him.

He stepped closer. Not out of hunger, though hunger was part of it. Not out of malice, for malice required intention he no longer possessed. He approached out of need, pure and simple and absolute. The emptiness inside him ached not for blood or flesh but for meaning, for the sensation of something mattering, for any feeling at all to fill the void the A'ta had left behind.

He knelt in the snow beside the root hollow. The squirrel's eyes found his, and for a moment they simply looked at each other. She knew what he was, recognized him in the way prey always recognized predator. But she could not flee, would not flee. To leave would be to abandon her young, and that was impossible for her. She would face him, face death itself, rather than leave them unprotected.

There was no violence in what happened next. He reached out, not with his hand but with something deeper, something that extended from the hollow place inside his chest. A reaching that preceded form. A tasting that required no mouth.

He touched her mind with something older than thought, more fundamental than language. And he drank.

Her love flooded him in impressions rather than images. The memory of sunlit moss where she had first felt safe. The joy of discovering a cache of acorns, the pleasure so intense it made her pause and simply experience gratitude. The fear of an owl's silent approach, the terror that sharpened every sense to painful clarity. The ache of protecting what was hers, the fierce determination that transcended self-preservation.

It poured into him, filling some of the emptiness but not all of it. Never all of it. The void inside him was too vast to be filled by one small life's accumulation of feeling. But it was something. After the terrible absence, it was everything.

And in return, he gave her something. Not deliberately, not as conscious trade or exchange, but because the taking created a vacuum that demanded filling. Dreams spilled from him into her, seeping through the same channel he had used to drink her memories.

She slept even as her eyes remained open, falling into a dream so deep and complete that nothing could wake her from it. In her dreaming, she saw a forest that never ended, where branches grew perpetually heavy with fruit that never rotted. No predators hunted there. No cold threatened. Her young were always fed, always safe, their bellies round and their eyes bright. The dream was soft and endless and empty of anything resembling truth.

It had no edges, no challenges, no growth. Just the same perfect moment repeated infinitely, comfort without end or meaning. She would never wake from it. Her body would continue its functions, her heart would beat, her lungs would draw breath. But her consciousness had gone somewhere else, somewhere he had created for her, and it would never return.

He stood slowly, the squirrel's memories settling inside him like stones dropped into still water. They did not fit comfortably. They pressed against the edges of the emptiness without filling it, creating an ache that was somehow worse than the original void had been. Now he knew what he was missing. Now he understood, in some fundamental way, what it meant to feel.

Inside him, something stirred. A flicker of warmth not his own. He could remember the shape of her nest now, rough and hastily constructed. He could recall the rhythm of her heartbeat, rapid and determined. He could taste her joy, faint and fleeting but real. These things belonged to him now, woven into whatever he was becoming.

He walked on, leaving the hollow behind. The three young would wake eventually, would find their mother unresponsive, would cry out in hunger and fear. They would not survive the cold without her active protection. But that knowledge did not reach him. He had taken what he needed and moved forward, because moving forward was what he did now.

Behind him, snow began to fall again, soft and relentless. The wind returned with gentle insistence, covering his tracks, hiding the hollow, erasing all evidence of what had transpired. The tundra exhaled, releasing the moment into the vast continuum of such moments, one more small tragedy absorbed into the endless cycle of taking and giving, living and dying, remembering and forgetting.

He walked through a world gone silent and strange. His footsteps made no sound now, or perhaps his ears no longer registered such things. The falling snow passed through him rather than landing on him, as if he had already begun to lose solidity, to become more idea than form.

The First Dream continued around him and through him. He was part of it now, no longer separate from the dreaming world but woven into its fabric. And somewhere in the vast whiteness ahead, other sleepers waited. Other lives hummed with feeling he could harvest. Other memories could be gathered and stored in the growing collection inside him.

He had become what the A'ta had made him. Not through intention or choice, but through the simple fact of emptiness seeking to be filled, of void calling to substance, of hunger finding at last a way to feed.

The First Dream was a hunger. A longing for memory before memory, for feeling before feeling. And though he did not understand it, though he possessed no framework for comprehending what he had become, the world had begun to remember him.

Not as N'Kai, for that name had been taken.

Not as human, for that form had been hollowed out.

As something new. Something that walked between life and dream, between taking and giving, between the world as it was and the world as it might be imagined.

He walked on through the endless white, and the First Dream walked with him.

CHAPTER 34

The Weight of Silence

The wind had changed.

It no longer whispered—it *carried.* A scent, faint and ancient, drifted across the tundra like a forgotten song. He followed it, though he did not know why. His feet moved without command, his body responding to something deeper than instinct. He had no hunger. No name. Only the ache of emptiness, and the squirrel's warmth still flickering inside him like a fading ember.

The land stretched wide and white, a canvas of stillness. The sky hung low, heavy with dusk, pressing against the horizon like a lid. The snow was not fresh—it was old, layered with memory, crusted with time. It crunched faintly beneath his boots, brittle and dry, like the cracking of ancient bones.

The air bit at his cheeks, sharp and metallic. The wind carried not just scent, but sound—low moans across the ice, the distant echo of something forgotten.

Then he saw it.

A shape, vast and unmoving, slumped at the edge of a frozen ravine. The mammoth.

Its body was half-buried in ice, fur tangled with frost and blood. One tusk was shattered, the other curved skyward like a monument to endurance. Its breath came slow, labored, each exhale a cloud that barely rose before vanishing.

He stood at a distance, watching. The mammoth's eyes were open, but dim. It neither flinched nor fled. It knew.

Around it, the snow bore the marks of struggle —wolf prints, claw gouges, the remnants of a battle already lost. The wolves were gone now, driven off or satisfied. But the mammoth remained. Alone. Waiting.

He stepped forward.

The snow parted beneath him, as if the tundra itself recognized the moment. He knelt beside the dying beast, his hands resting lightly on the ice.

The mammoth turned its head, just enough to meet his gaze.

And something passed between them.

Not words. Not thought. A recognition. The mammoth saw him—not as predator, not as kin, but as *vessel*. A being made to carry what others could no longer bear.

He reached out.

His fingers brushed the mammoth's brow, and the impressions surged.

He drank *memory*.

He saw green plains stretching beyond sight, herds moving like rivers, the rhythm of migration etched into the bones of the earth. He felt the weight of generations, the sorrow of calves lost to ice, the pride of survival. He heard songs sung in low thunder, passed from mother to child, from elder to sky.

The mammoth gave him everything.

And he, still unformed, still unnamed, *received*.

The impressions did not settle easily. They churned within him—vast, slow, mournful. He felt the ache of extinction, the dignity of endurance, the silence of being the last.

Though he did not understand the memories, they settled inside him like stones in a pond—heavy, quiet, permanent.

The mammoth's breath slowed.

He offered no dreams this time—only stillness. A silence deep enough to hold the mammoth's legacy without distortion. A space where memory could rest, unshaped, unforgotten.

The great beast exhaled one final time.

Its body stilled. Its eyes closed. The wind rose.

He remained kneeling long after the breath faded. The impressions churned within him—berries and thunder, nests and migrations. He did not know what he was becoming. Only that he was no longer empty.

He stood.

The wind howled now, louder than before. It lifted the mammoth's scent into the sky, scattering it like ash across the tundra.

He walked on.

Behind him, the snow began to fall again. Not in silence, but in rhythm.

And within him, the silence had shape. A rhythm. A beginning.

CHAPTER 35

The Edge of Bone

He did not cross the threshold into the village. Something held him back—an instinct or perhaps a recognition that he no longer belonged in such places. The village sprawled before him, built from the remains of mammoths long gone, their bones given new purpose in death. Ribs arched gracefully into doorways. Tusks had been carved into wind chimes that sang in gentle voices. Skulls stood hollowed into hearths where fires burned, the bone itself seeming to glow from within.

He stood beneath a leaning femur gate, half-shadowed by cedar branches and drifting snow. His breath came shallow. His hands hung empty at his sides, no longer certain what they were meant to hold.

Near the central fire pit, he saw her. A woman sat on a woven mat of sinew and reed, her hair silvered, her posture upright despite the years. In her lap, a child wriggled with restless energy, small limbs pushing against the embrace that held her.

The woman hummed a song older than the village, dipping a carved spoon into a bowl of thick stew. She brought it to the child's lips, blowing gently to cool the broth. The child accepted the food with complete trust. Small hands reached up for a strand of the woman's hair, wrapping the silver thread around tiny fingers. When it slipped free, the child giggled.

He could not look away. The scene pulled at something inside him, some part that remembered warmth and connection even though the specific memories had been stolen. He could not have said who she was, why she mattered, or even her name. But something in him recognized her nonetheless, the way an echo recognized the sound that created it.

He did not know she was his daughter, did not remember her birth beneath an eclipse or that Asha had whispered songs into her skin before vanishing. All of that had been taken from him.

But the body remembers what the mind forgets. His chest ached with pain that had no source. His hands trembled with the desire to reach out, though he did not know what he wanted to touch.

He watched the fire flicker in the child's eyes.

Watched the woman's hands move with love made habitual. Watched the village breathe around them, alive with the particular vitality that came from community.

A feather tied to the femur gate fluttered in the wind, then came loose, spiraling down to land at his feet. It was braided with rivergrass and mammoth hair and something dark that might have been human hair.

He stared at it for a long moment. He could not bring himself to touch it, though he could not have said why. Something about the feather felt too intimate, too connected to the world of the living.

He turned away from the gate. The movement cost him something. He felt it like a tearing, like roots being pulled from soil.

He walked into the deeper cold. Away from shelter and smoke and the sound of human voices. Away from the child who carried his blood without knowing his name.

Behind him, the village continued its evening rituals. The woman fed the child until the bowl was empty. The fires were banked. Voices called out final greetings.

The feather remained where it had fallen, slowly being covered by new snow.

He did not look back. The forest called to him from the distance. A presence vast and patient, waiting with the stillness of things that measured time in centuries. It offered what the village could not: a place where transformation could complete itself.

He walked toward it through the gathering darkness, leaving footprints that the snow quickly erased.

CHAPTER 36

The Worldforest

The forest rose before him like a wall of living memory, trees so vast their lower branches could shelter entire villages. The Worldforest stretched from one edge of the continent to the other, older than cities, older than stone, older than names.

He stood at its edge and felt it notice him. Not with sight or sound, but with something older. A recognition that passed between his hollow bones and roots that ran deeper than knowing. The forest breathed, and in that breath he heard both invitation and warning.

This was a threshold. Behind him lay the world of humans and their warm fires. Ahead lay something else entirely, something vast and patient and utterly inhuman in its scope.

He stepped forward, and the trees accepted him.

The moss beneath his feet glowed faintly, bioluminescent fungi creating pools of soft light. The trees leaned closer as he passed, their attention a weight he could feel. They recognized what he was becoming even if he did not yet understand it himself.

The forest whispered in a language older than words. It spoke through the smell of rich humus and the feel of bark. Through the particular quality of light filtered through layers of canopy. Through the presence of growing things pressing in from all sides.

It knew what he was. It knew what he would become.

He found the old tree without conscious searching. His feet simply carried him there, following paths that appeared beneath his steps and vanished behind him. The ancient being stood in a clearing that was not quite a clearing, its bark deeply furrowed, silver moss growing in patterns that seemed almost meaningful.

He approached slowly. When he finally reached the trunk, he rested his head against it, pressing his forehead to the cool bark.

The tree was solid beneath his touch, more real than anything else he had encountered since the A'ta had hollowed him. And the forest answered. Not with words or images, but with presence. With the simple overwhelming fact of being known.

He let go. Not of consciousness, but of the last desperate grip he'd maintained on his former self. The final threads connecting him to who he had been severed quietly, without drama or pain.

The forest held him as he dissolved. It caught him as he fell. And it began, with infinite patience, the long work of transforming him into something new.

CHAPTER 37

Dreaming

The forest absorbed him the way soil absorbs water, slowly and without resistance. His body settled against the base of the ancient tree, his back pressed to bark that had felt the passage of centuries.

The forest floor opened beneath him. Not dramatically, but gradually, inevitably. Roots shifted, creating space. The rich humus parted. Moss grew over his feet first, soft green tendrils creeping up his ankles with the patience of things that had no concept of hurry.

Time ceased to function in any recognizable way. The forest operated on its own schedule, measuring change not in the movement of sun across sky but in the slow turning of years into decades, decades into centuries.

The moss continued its climb, covering his legs, wrapping him in a blanket that was alive and breathing. Through that connection, he began to feel the forest's awareness, not as something separate but as an expansion of his own consciousness stretched across unimaginable distance.

His breathing slowed to match the forest's rhythm. His heartbeat followed, each pulse feeling like a season passing. Lichen grew across his shoulders. Small flowers bloomed in the moss that covered him, their roots drawing sustenance from his skin.

Birds nested in the crook of his arm. A fox denned near his feet. Mushrooms fruited from his shoulders in damp seasons, their caps opening like tiny umbrellas, releasing spores that drifted away.

He learned the language of growth by becoming growth itself. He understood how roots followed water because he could feel the pull of moisture through stone and soil. He comprehended how branches reached toward light because the yearning for sun was now his own yearning.

He learned the language of decay with equal intimacy. He felt fallen wood soften under patient work of bacteria and fungus. He experienced the transformation of death into nutrients, the way ending always fed beginning.

Birth and death became a single continuous process. His hunger, the desperate need that had driven him since the A'ta hollowed him out, faded into something closer to contentment. The forest filled him with the simple fact of existence, of being part of the endless cycle.

The moss claimed him entirely, covering him in a living shroud. His form became indistinct, less person and more presence. His consciousness expanded and thinned, spreading through the network of roots and mycelia until he touched the awareness of trees miles away.

The forest sang to him constantly, teaching what it meant to listen with patience measured in centuries, to wait with stillness that was more active than any human motion could ever be.

And through it all, he remained aware. Not conscious in the way humans were conscious, with their quick thoughts and faster feelings. But present. Witnessing.

He was being prepared, though for what he could not yet understand. The forest held him gently as the centuries passed, as kingdoms rose and fell beyond its borders, as languages were born and died.

And in the green dreaming depths of the Worldforest, beneath moss and lichen and the slow accumulation of seasons, he waited.

Hush, the forest whispered in its language

without words. Hush, and rest, and wait. Your time will come.

And he hushed. And rested. And waited.

CHAPTER 38

Dream's End

Eliria stepped into the clearing like dusk arriving—soft-footed, silver-eyed, her presence a hush rather than a call. She wore robes the color of twilight, fabric that seemed woven from shadow and starlight both, and her hair fell in a silver cascade down her back, threaded with small bones and feathers that clicked softly as she moved.

The branches parted for her as she entered. They opened out of recognition, the way old friends made room without being asked. She did not disturb the moss or startle the birds. She did not need to ask the forest to make space. It already had.

She moved like someone who had walked this path before—not recently, not often, but ritually. There was ceremony in her steps, in the way her fingers brushed against bark in passing, in the tilt of her head as she listened to what the trees were saying.

She paused at the edge of the clearing, taking in the sight of him. Moss had claimed him almost entirely, growing thick across his shoulders and down his arms in a living cloak of green. Lichen traced patterns across his chest like ancient script. Small white flowers bloomed in the tangle of his hair, their petals glowing faintly in the filtered light. His fingers had grown into the soil, roots threading between his knuckles, and his legs had fused with the earth so completely that it was hard to tell where his body ended and the forest floor began.

She approached slowly, reverently, as one might approach a shrine. When she reached him, she knelt in the soft humus beside him and brushed her fingers across the moss near his hand. The gesture was gentle, almost motherly. She did not try to wake him. She simply reminded him that he was not alone, that someone still remembered him, that the world beyond the dreaming still turned.

The moss responded beneath her touch, pulsing once like a heartbeat remembered. The bark above them sighed. A leaf detached from its branch and spiraled down through the canopy, catching light as it fell. A bird shifted on its perch but did not take flight, as if it too was waiting to see what would happen next.

She waited, neither patient nor impatient, simply present. The air around them thickened with meaning. The clearing held its breath. The forest leaned in.

And then he opened his eyes.

They were green-gold and clear, neither predator's eyes nor god's eyes. They were the eyes of someone just beginning to remember what it meant to be alive—to feel and want and choose rather than simply exist in the endless green dreaming.

***

He had expected to be a tree, or something like it. Still. Rooted. Slow. A thing that listened more than it spoke, a thing that did not need to choose.

He had slept beneath the great tree for so long that movement had become myth. Shape had become story. Self had become silence. The forest had held him like a lullaby—soft, repeating, ancient. A song sung in green and shadow.

It had fed him with feeling. Grief that hummed in the roots. Joy that curled in the moss. Silence so deep it echoed through his marrow. There had been no time there, only rhythm and breath and the slow unfolding of wonder.

He had become quiet because he was held. The forest had been a very good place to be. It did not ask him to be anything but present. It did not rush him toward purpose. It let him dissolve slowly, gently, into its rhythm.

There was joy there—the kind that waited rather than danced. The joy of leaf-light, of root-song, of moss that remembered every footstep and forgave them all. There was wonder too, the quiet astonishment of being allowed to exist.

So when he stirred—when the moss released him, when the bark above him sighed like a parent letting go—he expected to feel wood in his bones. Sap in his veins. Leaf-thoughts in his mind.

He expected to be slow, to be quiet, to be unchosen.

But he felt breath. He felt blood. He felt weight—the weight of knowing rather than branches.

He was a vessel, a shape made to carry what the forest could not say aloud.

The light touched his skin directly, warm and immediate. It startled him because it was new. He moved his fingers, and they did not root. They reached.

And that frightened him.

He was becoming. And that was harder, because trees did not choose. But he would.

***

She watched him breathe, just enough to prove he was no longer moss. The forest listened around them. The bark above held its breath. The moss beneath them curled inward, like a secret being kept.

Then, without urgency, she spoke.

"You were never asleep," she said. "You were listening."

Her voice was quiet, carrying the weight of someone who had spoken to trees and been answered. It did not echo. It settled.

"You are the echo of stillness. The breath of bark. The voice the forest could not shape alone." She placed her hand on the moss beside him, touching the memory of where he had been rather than him directly. "You are waking into the Second Dream, and it will ask more of you than silence."

She paused. The wind moved through the clearing like a thought trying to remember itself.

"The First Dream was stillness—the forest's dream, where you learned to listen. The Second Dream is motion. You will walk the world beyond these trees, gathering stories, sorrows, and small sacred things. You will learn what it means to carry others."

Her eyes held his, steady and clear.

"And when you have woven enough threads together—when you understand what binds soul to soul—you will be ready for the Third Dream. The dream of becoming whole."

She did not explain further. She simply waited, as if the words themselves were a door he must choose to walk through.

The forest exhaled. A leaf turned. A bird blinked but did not fly.

"You will find your name," she said softly. "You will walk as a bridge between what was and what will be. You will gather what others hold most dear. You will offer something in return, something they need without knowing. And slowly, thread by thread, you will become A'ta."

The word settled into the clearing like a stone into still water. A'ta. The gathered one. The keeper of threads.

"That is what you will be called," she said. "When you are ready."

And in the hush that followed, he felt the shape of her words settle into him as invitation rather than knowledge.

He did not speak at first. He turned his head slowly, like a leaf remembering wind, and looked at Eliria. Really looked. His gaze moved across her face, paused at her silver eyes, traced the line of her jaw. He was noticing rather than recognizing.

She did not smile or lean in. She simply remained, and that was enough.

He opened his mouth, just enough to let breath become sound.

"I..."

Then stopped. Because it was a shape, a feeling, a thread pulling him forward rather than a memory.

He tried again. "I..."

He looked down at his hands. They were his, neither bark nor root.

He flexed his fingers. They reached instead of digging.

He closed his eyes to listen, and the forest whispered its letting go.

He opened his eyes again.

"I'm afraid," he said.

Eliria did not answer immediately. She placed her hand on the moss beside his again, and her breath caught just slightly. A flicker of something passed across her face—sympathy, perhaps, or memory.

"I know," she finally said.

The wind moved through the clearing like a breath held too long. A bird blinked. A leaf turned. The forest exhaled.

And he sat up—not quickly, not fully, just enough to begin becoming.

CHAPTER 39

Stillwater

That night, the hush song did not end. It folded into the reeds, into the mud, into the breath between dragonfly wings. It lingered in the curve of the heron's neck, wound through the willow's roots, and dissolved into the darkness between stars.

The heron slept on, head tucked beneath its wing. The willow's branches hung motionless in the windless air.

But something inside him began to take shape, slowly and without clarity. Just enough to stir the stillness—a tremor in deep water, a seed splitting underground.

He sat beside the pool until the stars wheeled overhead and faded, until the wind died to nothing, until the hush became a kind of gravity pulling him down and holding him steady.

The vibration in his palm had faded, but its echo remained—a word waiting to be spoken, hovering on the edge of thought. A thread connecting what was to what might be.

He did not remember who he had been. The past was a door sealed shut, a room he could no longer enter.

He did not know what he would become. The future stretched before him, formless and vast.

But the silence around him felt familiar, the way a scar remembers the knife.

The water held still, its surface dark as obsidian beneath the starlight. It received him the way earth accepts rain, without resistance or question.

He reached out, fingers trembling, and touched the surface. It did not ripple. It did not resist. It simply remained, cool and ancient against his skin.

"Stillwater," he said, just loud enough for the word to exist.

The word tasted of mud and moonlight, of depths he could not fathom.

The name did not answer. It accepted.

And something inside him aligned—a key turning in a lock he hadn't known existed. A root finding soil after a long fall through darkness.

He was not healed. The wounds still ached beneath his skin.

He was not whole. Too many pieces remained scattered and lost.

But he was named.

And the Second Dream could begin—not with fire blazing across the sky or wings carrying him above the world, but with stillness that had learned to listen to the song beneath the song. With silence that had learned to carry weight without breaking. With a name that invited rather than demanded, a door left open, a path appearing in mist.

Stillwater. The place where memory rests beneath the surface. The place where becoming begins, slow and certain as the turning of seasons.

Eliria stood at the edge of the clearing, watching him name himself. She did not interrupt. She did not congratulate. She simply witnessed, as she had witnessed others before him, as she would witness others after.

When he looked up at her, she nodded once.

"Now," she said, "your teaching begins."

The forest around them stirred, branches creaking softly in a breeze that had not been there moments before. Somewhere in the canopy, a bird began to sing—hesitant at first, then gaining confidence, its melody threading through the green shadows.

He stood slowly, his legs remembering how to bear weight, his body remembering how to move through space as something separate from the earth. The moss that had covered him fell away in soft clumps. The flowers in his hair withered and dropped, their petals scattering across the forest floor like snow.

He was no longer part of the dreaming. He was awake, and aware, and afraid.

But he was named. And that would have to be enough.

Eliria turned and began to walk deeper into the forest. After a moment's hesitation, he followed, his footsteps uncertain on ground that felt both familiar and strange. The trees leaned in as he passed, their branches forming an archway above him, and he could feel their attention like a weight on his shoulders.

He had been held by the forest for centuries. Now it was letting him go.

The First Dream was over. The Second Dream had begun.

And somewhere ahead, in the green shadows where light filtered through leaves like stained glass, his future waited—patient and inevitable as the turning of the world.

CHAPTER 40

The Teaching

He did not know how long he had walked before Eliria began to teach him. Time in the Worldforest was counted in silences—in the hush between frog calls, in the way the willow roots shifted when no wind moved. She taught slowly, with presence rather than words.

The first village appeared at dusk, nestled against the forest's edge like a child against its mother's side. Eliria stopped at the tree line, her hand light on his shoulder.

"Watch," she said.

They waited until the cooking fires dimmed and the voices faded, until the only sounds were crickets and the soft breathing of sleep. She led him to a window where a child slept, her face turned toward the moonlight. Eliria knelt beside the sill, her fingers hovering above the child's temple, never quite touching.

"Do you see it?" Eliria whispered.

He saw nothing. Only the child's peaceful face, her small chest rising and falling.

"The shine," Eliria said. "Watch the edges of her dream."

Then he saw it—a faint shimmer, like heat rising from summer stones. It curled from the child's sleeping form, gossamer-thin, catching the moonlight.

"Memory-light," Eliria said. "Every soul sheds it in sleep, when the mind loosens its grip."

She reached out, and the shimmer drifted toward her palm like a moth to flame. Her fingers closed gently around it. The light condensed, became solid—a thread no thicker than spider silk, glowing softly between her thumb and forefinger.

She brought it to her lips and inhaled. The thread dissolved into her, a shimmer that traveled beneath her skin like light through water.

The child stirred but did not wake.

"Now you," Eliria said.

His hand trembled. The shimmer recoiled from him.

"She feels your hunger," Eliria said. "You must be gentler than sleep itself."

He breathed the way Eliria breathed—slow,

patient, inevitable as nightfall. This time the shimmer drifted closer. When it touched his palm, warmth flooded through him. The taste of honey bread. A grandmother's weathered hands. The sound of a familiar song.

He drew it to his lips. It dissolved on his tongue—honey and song and the warmth of weathered hands—then sank into him.

The child's smile faded.

"What did you take?" he whispered.

"A morning with her grandmother," Eliria said. She drew another thread—sharper, brighter. "I took the day her father returned from war."

"But—"

"And I left this." Eliria leaned close and breathed out softly. Where her breath touched, new shimmer formed—golden, warm, impossibly sweet.

"Not a real memory. A dream of being cherished. Of safety."

The child's face transformed. Her smile returned, deeper than before. Radiant.

"She feels joy," Stillwater whispered.

"More than joy," Eliria said. "Bliss. Ecstasy. The sweetness we leave is more intense than any real memory could be."

He asked if it was kindness. She said nothing.

He asked if it was theft. She said, "It is becoming."

She made him practice on sleepers at the forest's edge. Travelers. Hunters. Those who camped alone beneath the stars.

At first, he could only gather the faintest threads—surface dreams, shallow memories. The scent of bread baking. The sound of rain on leaves.

"Deeper," Eliria said.

He reached further and touched something sharp—a man's memory of battle. The copper tang of blood. The weight of a dying friend.

Stillwater recoiled. The thread snapped back into the sleeper.

"You flinched," Eliria said. "Pain is the brightest thread. It will call to you most strongly. You must take what shines, not what you wish to take."

She drew out the battle-memory and breathed it in. Light pulsed beneath her skin. Then she breathed out a dream of absolution, of forgiveness.

"He will wake believing he has been pardoned,"

she said. "He will sleep deeply tomorrow night, hoping to feel it again."

Stillwater stared at his own hands. "We're feeding them lies."

"We're feeding them hunger," Eliria said. "The sweetness we leave is bait. The more they taste it, the more they offer us in sleep."

And when sleep was not enough, she showed him how to draw from the waking. She drew grief from a woman still awake, speaking of her daughter who had passed. The shimmer rose from her skin as she wept. Eliria gathered it gently, breath by breath, until the woman glowed with joy she could not explain.

Tomorrow, she would wonder why she couldn't quite recall her daughter's face. But she would chase that feeling. She would do anything to feel it again.

***

Seasons passed, or what felt like seasons in the timeless forest.

Stillwater grew skilled. The shimmer came to him willingly now, recognizing him as predator and provider both. He learned to taste memories before taking them, to sort the threads by weight and brightness, to craft the sweetness he left behind to compel rather than comfort.

A widow dreamed of her husband's touch and woke aching for it. A soldier tasted false valor and could not bear his waking shame. A lonely farmer found friendship in sleep and withdrew from the living.

They came back. Again and again. Offering more. Fading slowly.

One evening, as mist rose from the stillwater pool, Eliria finally spoke.

"You are A'ta now," she said. "Walker of the Second Dream."

He had suspected, but hearing it named made it real.

"What is the Third Dream?" he asked.

"To become A'ta is to walk the Second Dream and prepare for the Third Dream. The Third Dream requires a soul woven from the finest threads—memories and emotions crystallized into something new."

"A soul for whom?"

"For the one who comes after."

"You are no longer the vessel," she said. "You are the weaver."

He understood. They were gathering for something yet unborn, something that would inherit all these stolen, beautiful fragments.

"Will I meet them?" he asked.

"Some do. Most do not. The weaving takes lifetimes."

She placed a hand over his heart and hummed a melody he had never heard—low and ancient, wordless and full of longing.

He wept without knowing why.

***

She left before dawn, while he still slept beside the stillwater pool.

There was no farewell. No final lesson. No gift.

She stood. She turned. She walked into the trees. And the forest did not mark her passing.

He woke to silence. The hush song had faded. The willow roots no longer whispered her name.

He did not call for her. He did not search. He knew. It was the way of the A'ta. They came to shape. They stayed to teach. They left when the vessel became the weaver.

Stillwater stood at the forest's edge, feeling the weight of the gathered threads woven into himself—hundreds of them now, each one a fragment of joy or sorrow, courage or fear.

Above him, the stars were fading into morning. Somewhere beyond the trees, people were waking lighter than they should be, glowing with false bliss that would make them hunger for true feeling they could no longer name.

And somewhere, in a future he could not yet imagine, someone would inherit everything he gathered.

He touched his chest where the threads lived beneath his skin. They hummed softly, a harmony of harvested moments and planted hunger.

The Second Dream had begun.

He turned toward the nearest village and began to walk.

CHAPTER 41

Interlude: The Years He Walked

He walked before the years had names, before humans marked their seasons with numbers or carved their calendars into stone. Time moved differently for him now. It flowed not as a river moving forward but as a vast stillness he moved through, touching moments the way a hand trails through water without disturbing the current beneath.

The Second Dream had no end, only continuation. He walked and gathered, gave and took, and the centuries accumulated inside him like sediment settling at a river's bed. Layer upon layer of memory, sorrow, and small sacred things that others could no longer bear to carry.

* * *

The snowfields stretched endless and white beneath a sky the color of old bone. Here the last mammoths still walked, their great shapes moving through the drifts like ships through frozen seas. Stillwater found the child at the edge of a ravine where the wind had carved the snow into ridges sharp as blades.

She could not have been more than six winters old, her small body wrapped in furs that had once belonged to someone larger. A man's furs, cut down and stitched to fit her narrow shoulders. She sat motionless in the snow, staring at a tusk necklace clutched in her raw-red fingers. The cold had turned her lips blue, but she did not seem to notice. She was too busy trying to remember.

Stillwater crouched beside her, close enough to see the frost forming on her eyelashes. The memory-light rose from her in wisps of pale gold, carrying fragments of a voice she was losing, a face that blurred more with each passing day. Her father had died in the hunt three moons past, and now she could not recall the sound of his laughter. She remembered that he had laughed, remembered that the sound had made her feel safe, but the laughter itself had slipped away like water through cupped hands.

The grief was too heavy for such small shoulders. It pressed her into the snow, pinned her there with its impossible weight. She had stopped eating. She had stopped speaking. She had come to this ravine to join her father in whatever silence waited beyond the cold.

Stillwater reached out and let his fingers hover near her temple. The memory-light drifted toward him, drawn by the emptiness he carried. He gathered it gently: the weight of absence, the ache of forgetting, the desperate love that had nowhere left to go. It tasted of salt and woodsmoke and the particular sweetness of a child's adoration.

And in its place, he breathed a dream.

The child's eyes fluttered closed. In the dream he gave her, there was a fire that never died and arms that wrapped around her with perfect warmth. There was a voice. Not her father's voice exactly, but a voice that carried the same quality of safety, the same promise that she was loved and would always be loved. The dream held no specific memories because he could not return what he had taken. But it held feeling, pure and distilled, the essence of comfort without the pain of loss.

When her eyes opened again, the blue had faded from her lips. She blinked at the snow around her as if waking from a long sleep, then stood on legs that no longer trembled. She could not remember why she had come to this place or what she had been mourning. She only knew that somewhere inside her chest, a warmth had kindled that the cold could not touch.

She walked back toward the distant smoke of her village, leaving the tusk necklace half-buried in the snow. Stillwater watched her go, then gathered the necklace and held it against his chest. The ivory was cold and smooth, worn from years of touching. He added it to the collection he carried. Not of objects, but of the weight they represented. Another thread woven into the tapestry of what he was becoming.

* * *

The caves came later, though how much later he could not say. Time had begun to blur at its edges, one century bleeding into the next like watercolors left in rain.

He found the boy deep in the earth's belly, where torchlight flickered against walls that had never known sun. The air hung thick with the smell of animal fat and ground pigment, of smoke and stone and the particular mustiness of places long enclosed. Water dripped somewhere in the darkness, each drop a small percussion that echoed through chambers carved by millennia of patient erosion.

The boy knelt before a wall smooth as skin, his hands trembling as they moved. He was perhaps twelve summers old, his body balanced on the edge between childhood and something harder. Red ochre stained his fingers to the wrist. Black charcoal smudged his cheeks where he had wiped sweat or tears. Before him, horses ran across the stone. They were not merely painted but alive somehow, their legs stretched in eternal gallop, their manes flowing in a wind that existed only in pigment and faith.

But the boy was not painting horses now. His hand moved in curves that did not match any creature Stillwater had seen. The shapes folded and rose, suggesting wings where no wings belonged. The boy was painting something he had dreamed, something that existed nowhere but in the private country of his imagination. His whole body trembled with the effort of translation, of forcing the vision in his mind through his clumsy fingers and onto the unforgiving stone.

The memory-light that rose from him was brilliant, almost blinding. It carried the particular intensity of absolute belief: the certainty that the world was larger than what could be seen, that stone could hold spirit, that a boy with pigment-stained hands could reach across the boundary between real and imagined and bring something back.

Stillwater approached slowly, his shadow falling across the painted horses. The boy did not turn, too consumed by his work to notice anything beyond the wall before him. His breathing came ragged and fast. His torch was guttering, nearly spent. He had been here for hours, perhaps days, painting until his fingers cramped and his vision blurred.

The awe rose from him like heat from sun-warmed stone. Stillwater gathered it with cupped hands, drew it into himself through the space between breaths. It tasted of mineral and darkness, of the profound wonder that came from understanding, even briefly, that the world was stranger and more beautiful than anyone had taught him to believe.

In return, Stillwater gave him flight.

The dream he breathed into the boy's sleeping mind was simple: wings beating against painted stars, the cave's ceiling falling away to reveal an endless sky, the sensation of rising and rising until the earth below became a memory and the wind became home. It was not the awe he had taken, for that particular feeling could never be returned once harvested. But it was something to fill the space, a sweetness that would make the boy return to his paintings again and again, chasing the shadow of a feeling he could no longer name.

When the boy woke, his torch had died. He sat in absolute darkness, surrounded by paintings he could no longer see. But he was smiling. And somewhere deep in his chest, something had shifted. A hunger kindled that would drive him back to these caves until his hair turned gray, painting creatures no one else could see, trying to recapture a wonder that had slipped away in the night.

* * *

The river settlements rose with the warming of the world. Where once ice had stretched unbroken, now water flowed and reeds grew thick along muddy banks. Humans gathered where the fishing was good, built shelters of woven grass and clay, planted seeds in soil dark with centuries of accumulated richness.

Stillwater walked among them as twilight settled over the water. The air smelled of cook fires and river mud, of grain being ground between stones that had been worn smooth by generations of hands. Voices carried across the settlement: laughter, argument, the particular rhythms of a community settling into evening.

He found the girl at the river's edge, her feet bare in the shallows. She was young, perhaps ten summers, with hair that hung loose and tangled to her waist. Her hands moved through the water as she hummed, tracing patterns in the current that seemed almost purposeful. The song she hummed was not hers. She did not know this, but Stillwater recognized it immediately. The cadence, the particular way certain notes bent toward others. It was her grandmother's song, learned in the years before language, absorbed through skin and bone while she slept in the old woman's arms.

The grandmother had died two winters past. The girl had wept then, had felt the loss like a wound that would not heal. But time had gentled the grief, and now she hummed the song without knowing where it came from, without remembering the weathered hands that had first shaped those notes, the voice that had sung them into her sleeping ears.

The memory-light rose from her in threads of silver and gold, carrying the weight of inheritance. The rhythm of hands teaching hands, the sound of voices passing songs from generation to generation. It was precious beyond measure, this unconscious continuation of the dead through the living.

Stillwater gathered it with the gentleness such things required. He took the rhythm, the knowledge that lived in her body rather than her mind, the inheritance she carried without understanding. It dissolved on his tongue like honey mixed with ash.

The dream he left was river-born: water that sang back to her in voices she could almost recognize, currents that wrapped around her ankles like welcoming hands, the sensation of being part of something larger that stretched back before her birth and would continue after her death. It was not the same as knowing her grandmother's song. But it was something. A comfort that would draw her back to this river again and again, searching for a connection she could no longer name.

When the girl returned to her family's shelter that night, she had forgotten the melody. She tried to hum it and found only silence where the notes should have been. But she was smiling, and when she slept, she dreamed of water that knew her name.

* * *

The shell islands rose from warm seas in latitudes Stillwater had never walked before. Here the dead were mourned with fire and salt, their bodies given to flames while their families stood at the water's edge and wept. The smoke rose in columns that leaned with the wind, carrying the scent of burning driftwood and sacred herbs, of flesh returning to air and ash returning to sea.

The man had been kneeling at the shore for three days.

His wife's pyre had burned to nothing on the first night, the flames consuming her body while he watched with eyes that had forgotten how to blink. On the second day, the tide had carried the last of her ashes into the deeper water. Now, on the third day, he knelt on shells that had worn smooth from centuries of mourning, and he could not remember why he remained.

He had not eaten. He had not spoken. He had not moved except to breathe, and even that seemed like more effort than he could sustain. His grief was a weight that pressed him into the shells, that threatened to crush the breath from his lungs. He wanted to follow his wife into the sea, to dissolve the way she had dissolved, to become salt and foam and memory.

But he could not remember her laugh.

This was what tortured him most. Not her death, for death came to everyone, the sea took all things eventually. What tortured him was the forgetting that had already begun. Her face remained clear in his mind, the particular way she had tilted her head when listening, the strength in her hands when she worked the nets. But her laugh, that sound that had made him fall in love with her twenty summers past, had slipped away. He knew she had laughed often. He knew the sound had been beautiful. But the laugh itself had gone, and no amount of grieving could bring it back.

Stillwater approached across the shells, each step crunching softly in the pre-dawn quiet. The man did not look up. He had gone somewhere beyond noticing, beyond the world of the living and not yet arrived in the world of the dead.

The memory-light that rose from him was blue-white with pain, so bright it hurt to witness. Stillwater gathered it carefully, drawing out the weight of silence, the impossibility of a world that continued without her. He could not take the love, for that ran too deep, was woven too completely through the man's being. But he could take the edges of it, the sharpest parts that cut rather than comforted.

The dream he left was water and light: waves that whispered her name in voices the man could almost recognize, sunlight on the sea surface that shifted into the shape of her smile, the sensation of her presence nearby, watching, still loving him from whatever shore she had reached. It was not true. She was gone, dissolved into elements that would never reassemble. But the dream gave him permission to stand, to eat, to continue living in a world that had briefly seemed unendurable.

When the man rose on the morning of the fourth day, his knees ached from the shells and his stomach cramped with hunger. But his eyes held a light they had lacked before, a soft, false hope that would carry him through the years to come. He would search for that feeling again, would spend long hours at the water's edge, waiting for the waves to whisper her name. But he would live. And that was something, even if it was not quite healing.

* * *

The steppes stretched to horizons that seemed to curve with the world's turning. Here grass grew thick and golden, rippling in winds that never ceased, and horses ran in herds so vast their hooves made the earth itself tremble. The people who lived here measured wealth in animals and honor, in the glory won through courage and the shame avoided through strength.

Stillwater found the young warrior at his brother's grave.

The burial mound rose from the grassland like a gentle wave frozen mid-swell. Inside lay bones adorned with gold, weapons that would never again taste battle, and the skeleton of a horse that had followed its master into death. The grave goods told a story of valor, a man who had died well, who had earned his place among the honored dead.

But the young man kneeling at the mound's base had not died well. He had not died at all. This was his shame, his unbearable burden. He had survived the battle that claimed his brother. He had lived while better men fell around him.

And now he knelt in the grass, his face pressed to the earth, trying to understand why the gods had chosen to spare the lesser brother while taking the greater.

His fear rose from him in waves. Not fear of death, for death would have been welcome, but fear of a life lived in his brother's shadow. Fear that he would never prove worthy. Fear that when his time came to face the final battle, he would fail again, would flee when he should stand firm, would survive when he should sacrifice.

Stillwater settled beside him in the grass. The wind moved around them both, carrying the scent of distant rain and sun-warmed earth. The young man did not stir. His breathing came in ragged gasps that might have been sobs, if warriors were permitted to weep.

The memory-light was shot through with darkness, shame and fear braided together so tightly they could not be separated. Stillwater gathered what he could, drawing out the heaviest strands, the ones that threatened to crush the young man beneath their weight. He took the memory of his brother's final cry, the image of his body falling, the sound of laughter that would never echo across the camp again.

The dream he gave in return was endless riding. Sky and grass without boundary, the thunder of hooves beneath him, the wind in his face as he galloped toward a horizon that never arrived. And beside him, always beside him, a figure that might have been his brother, that might have been himself, that might have been the warrior he had always hoped to become. They rode together through fields of gold, neither leading nor following, simply moving as one through a world without shame or shadow.

When the young man lifted his face from the earth, his eyes were dry and his jaw was set. He could not remember exactly what had driven him to this mound or what he had been mourning. He knew only that somewhere inside him, a fire had kindled. A need to ride, to prove, to become something worthy. He mounted his horse and rode east toward battles that waited beyond the horizon, chasing a feeling of reunion he could never quite grasp.

* * *

The temple had been abandoned for a generation when Stillwater found it. Olive trees grew through the broken floor, their roots splitting the ancient stones as they reached for water beneath. Columns lay toppled among wildflowers. The altar had cracked down its center, leaving a gap through which small creatures made their homes.

But people still came here. Not to worship, for

the gods this place had honored were forgotten now, their names erased from living memory. They came to hope. They believed the old stones held power, that prayers whispered among the ruins might reach ears that prayers spoken elsewhere could not find.

The woman knelt before the broken altar, her belly swollen with child. She was perhaps thirty summers old, though the lines around her eyes suggested she had lived each of those summers hard. Her hands were calloused from work, her dress patched and faded from years of washing. But her face held the particular luminosity of hope, of desperate faith that refused to dim despite all evidence that the world was not kind to prayers.

She had come seeking a vision for her unborn child. She wanted to know if the baby would survive, if it would be strong, if it would live a life better than her own. She had lost three children already. Two to fever, one to the hunger that came in the year the crops failed. This child, she believed, would be different. Had to be different. She had walked two days to reach this place, had slept among the broken columns and eaten nothing but the olives that grew from the temple's bones.

Her hope rose from her in strands of gold so bright they seemed to illuminate the ruined space. It was fragile, that hope. Trembling and uncertain, bruised by loss but not yet broken. Stillwater approached slowly, stepping over roots and fallen stone. The woman's eyes were closed, her lips moving in prayers to gods who could no longer hear.

He gathered her hope with particular care. It was precious, this capacity to believe despite evidence, to trust in futures that had no guarantee. He took the weight of her expecting, the fierce maternal certainty that this child would be the one who survived, who thrived, who made all the grief worthwhile.

The dream he left was sunlight through olive leaves: a child laughing beneath branches heavy with fruit, small hands reaching for hers with complete trust, the sound of a voice calling her name with the particular inflection of love. It was not prophecy, for he could not see the future, could not promise that her child would survive or that her life would ease. But it was comfort, a sweetness that filled the hollow place where hope had been.

When she opened her eyes, the sun had moved across the sky and shadows pooled in the temple's broken corners. She did not remember why she had come here or what she had prayed for. She only knew that somewhere deep in her belly, where the baby stirred and kicked, she felt a warmth that had not been there before. She rose and began the long walk home, one hand pressed to her swollen middle, smiling at nothing in particular.

* * *

The centuries accumulated like sediment in his veins.

He walked through kingdoms that rose and fell like waves against a shore. He watched cities build themselves from nothing and crumble back to dust. He gathered memory from emperors and beggars, from conquerors and conquered, from the celebrated and the forgotten. Each thread added to the tapestry of what he was becoming, each stolen hope and borrowed grief woven into something vast and patient and only partially human.

Languages were born and died around him. He learned to speak in tongues that would not exist for centuries more, then forgot them as they faded from living mouths. He watched the same stories told and retold across generations, watched the same fears shape the same faces, watched humanity circle through patterns as old as hunger and as inevitable as loss.

The threads inside him sang with accumulated weight. Grief beyond counting. Joy beyond measure. The sum of human feeling across millennia, compressed into a vessel that walked on two legs and remembered everything and nothing at once.

And still he walked. Still he gathered. Still he gave the sweetness that made them return, that made them offer more and more of themselves in exchange for dreams that tasted like truth but held no substance.

The world changed around him, but the hunger remained constant. The need to fill the emptiness, to weave the threads into something whole, to prepare for the one who would inherit everything he gathered. This purpose carried him forward through centuries that blurred into one long, continuous moment of becoming.

* * *

He walked into Maine when brother fought brother and the nation split like heartwood.

The war had not touched this place directly. No battles scarred the landscape, no armies had marched through the snow-silent pines. But its shadow lay over everything nonetheless, darkening the faces of those who remained while their sons and brothers and husbands fought and died in places with names that meant nothing and everything at once.

The farmhouse sat alone at the edge of the forest, its clapboards weathered gray by decades of harsh winters. Smoke rose from the chimney in a thin column that the wind immediately scattered. The surrounding fields lay fallow under early snow, waiting for a spring planting that might never come if the war took everyone who remained to work them.

Stillwater found the girl in the loft where she had retreated to read her letter for the hundredth time. She was perhaps sixteen, her hair the color of autumn wheat, her fingers ink-stained from writing responses that took weeks to arrive and often went unanswered. The letter in her hands was three weeks old, its paper soft from repeated handling, its creases threatening to tear.

Her brother had written from somewhere in Virginia. He had described the food, which was terrible, and the weather, which was worse, and he had not described the fighting at all. He had asked about their father's health, about the cow that had been sick when he left, about the early frost that had threatened the apple crop. He had not asked if she was well because asking would have meant acknowledging that she might not be, that waiting was its own kind of wound.

She did not know if he still breathed. The letter was already old when it arrived, and that was weeks ago now. He could be dead already, buried in soil he had never seen, and she would not know for months more. The uncertainty was worse than grief would have been. Grief, at least, was certain. This waiting was a wound that could not heal because it could not close.

Her anguish rose from her in strands of silver shot through with red, the color of waiting, of suspended love, of hope that had curdled into fear but refused to release into despair. Stillwater moved through the shadows of the loft, careful not to disturb the hay or the mice that nested in its warmth. The girl did not notice him. She was too far gone into the letter, reading words she had memorized weeks ago, searching for meaning that was not there.

He gathered the weight of her waiting with hands that had grown practiced over millennia. He took the sleepless nights spent listening for hoofbeats that might bring news. He took the meals she could not eat, the prayers she could not finish, the desperate bargaining with a god she was no longer sure existed. He took the particular torture of loving someone who might already be gone, of not knowing whether to grieve or hope or simply endure.

The dream he left was simple and profound: a clearing in the pines behind her father's farm, where snow lay soft and unmarked, and footsteps approached from the tree line. Her brother's face emerging from the shadows, thin but alive, tired but whole. His arms opening to receive her. The smell of pine and snow and home, of safety restored, of ending that was also beginning.

He breathed the dream into her sleeping mind as darkness fell over the farm. It settled into her like warmth spreading from a hearth, filling the hollow places where fear had lived, replacing the sharp edges of uncertainty with something soft and sweet and completely false.

When she woke the next morning, the letter still lay in her lap, but she could not remember why it had frightened her so. A lightness had entered her chest where weight had been. She descended the ladder from the loft and ate breakfast with her father for the first time in weeks, and when he asked what had changed, she could only say that she had dreamed of Thomas coming home.

But the dream did not fade the way dreams usually did. It lingered in her bones, in the corners of her vision. It called to her from the tree line, from the shadows between the pines. After breakfast, she found herself standing at the edge of the forest, looking into its green-black depths, feeling the inexplicable certainty that something waited for her there.

She stepped past the first trees. Then the second. Then the third.

The snow swallowed her footprints as she walked, erasing her passage as if she had never been. The pines leaned in around her, their branches interlocking overhead until the sky became a memory. The scent of moss and cold and something older filled her lungs, and she breathed it in without fear.

Deep in the forest, in a clearing that existed between one world and another, Stillwater waited. The threads inside him hummed with accumulated weight: millennia of gathered memory, of sorrow and joy and all the complicated feelings that lay between. He did not know why this girl, why this moment, why this particular clearing in these particular pines.

The girl emerged from the trees with snow in her wheat-colored hair and a smile on her lips that did not quite match her eyes. She looked at him without fear, without surprise, as if she had always known he would be there.

And the forest, ancient and patient, held its breath.

* * *

END OF PART ONE

www.ingramcontent.com/pod-product-compliance
Lightning Source LLC
LaVergne TN
LVHW090513110826
845146LV00003B/835

* 9 7 9 8 9 9 3 1 4 8 3 1 1 *